Felix Publishing 2018
www.felixpublishing.com.au
email: info@felixpublishing.com
Print copies available from publisher.

Letters from San Rafael

2018 digital book release
ISBN: 978-0-9946433-8-4
Second Print Edition
ISBN: 978-0-9946433-9-1
Author: Dr Peter T. Scott (as Hernán Eduardo Moreno Ruiz)

Registration:
Thorpe-Bowker +61 3 8517 8342
email: bowkerlink@thorpe.com.au

This is a work of fiction. The characters in this book did not exist and the politics of the time has been generalized. Some of the places described are real and are well-known to the author. No disrespect is meant to any people living or dead in the countries of South America for which the author has a great love.

Letters
From
San Rafael

Hernán Moreno Ruiz

Compiled by Dr. Peter T. Scott

To my grandchildren who are yet
to travel to the high places

Contents

Introduction

In troubled times we are often judged not by the stories told about us, but by the stories we are able to tell. So it is that this book is about two men and the stories which they have told in the letters from San Rafael.

The time in which these stories are told is that transition period in South America, some sixty years after the great liberators, Bolivar, San Martin, O'Higgins and Sucre. Despite the fact that independence has been gained and new nations re-forged from the old colonies of Spain, the rivalries and jealousies of the past still remain. National borders are drawn and re-drawn as these new nations fight over land and territory. Often these borders are drawn though the traditional lands of the peoples who have lived there for centuries. Old family territories are divided and members of the family now belong to the whims of several governments. But just as their beloved mountains remain, so the people of the land continue in their daily lives in this harsh land. The old trade routes which once followed the footpaths of the Incas and their ancestors are still used, but the honest traders are now called smugglers. Life goes on; only the names of the lords of the land change.

The two men who tell these tales are vastly different from each other and are in themselves examples of the peoples who lived in these times. Hernán Eduardo Moreno Ruiz, the author of these letters is a university lecturer in philosophy who volunteered for the Peruvian Militia as a young student in an early time of border tension. In time he became a Teniente Coronel[1]. He would say that he did not do this out of patriotism but rather in support of his friends who were conscripted whilst he was given exemption. ¿Quién sabe? - who knows? Certainly one could point out that at that time his country was yet again threatened by their northern neighbours, also that the young Hernán's grandfather, Bernardo Moreno Fuentes, had died leading his battalion at the Battle of Ayacucho in 1824 during the Wars of Independence. But these accusations would be dismissed by the quiet academic who would say that history has shown that heroes are made by the circumstances not by the intension of the man.

[1] Lieutenant Colonel.

The other man is the complete opposite. Pablo Garcia was a tough, regular soldier in the Ejército del Perú[2]. He had left his family's poor farm in the high mountains of northern Peru and had walked to the nearest town to join the army. He too would scoff at any hints of patriotism and say in his simple and direct way of speaking, that poverty makes every person a potential hero. In time, his natural intelligence and ability to lead men in battle gained the poorly-educated peasant his rank of Sargento Primero[3].

The vastly different lives of these two men finally converged in 1882 during the disastrous War of the Pacific. At that time, Chile had annexed the coastal territory of Bolivia for its mineral wealth.

[2] The Army of Peru.
[3] First Sergeant (Warrant Officer).

Peru had entered this war on the side of Bolivia but both were soundly beaten by the more militant and organised Chile. Bolivia lost its coastline and Peru was invaded. Comandante[4] Moreno was then an administrative officer in the 5th Mountain Brigade and a Senior Lecturer at the Universidad Nacional de San Antonio Abad[5] in his hometown of Cuzco. He held this Militia appointment now on full-time duty for two reasons; firstly because he was a gifted administrator and secondly because he had long been an outspoken critic of his superior officers in their use of outmoded tactics and treatment of the common soldier. With the city of Puno in the south of Peru being threatened by the

[4] Major

[5] The University of Saint Anthony the Abbot – the oldest and largest university in Cuzco.

Chileans and the remnants of his army now fleeing north into the rugged hills beyond Lake Titicaca, he was finally given command of a company of men to march south and assist in the reorganisation of Peru's defence. Comandante Moreno had no doubts that this was a fruitless adventure. Never-the-less he had gathered a mixture of administrative staff, new conscripts and patriotic volunteers and marched south. The three hundred kilometre route was along the old road through the high valleys which connected Cuzco, the capital of the old Incan Empire to its traditional heartland on the lake. For Hernán Moreno, this journey had personal significance for his mother, Doña Valentina Ruiz Yupanqui, could trace her ancestry back to the Capac Incans, the highest rank of the nobility of the ancient Incan peoples. Hernán's father, Fernando Hernán Moreno Lopez, a minor politician had died when he was only five years of age and so he was raised by his mother with the help of her brothers who often told of the myths and legends of the peoples of the Andes. A quiet, studious boy without siblings, Hernán had loved to visit his uncles and his many cousins who lived in Cuzco or in the mountains on their modest estates. Here he could be free and walk the valleys of the altiplano[6] with his cousins and talk to the Andinos[7] whose lives were very different from that in the city.

The Sargento and the Comandante met near the village of Pucara just north of the Lake. Garcia had collected the remnants of his men after most of his

---

[6] The high plains within the mountains of the Andes.
[7] Name used in this book collectively for the peoples of the Andes.

officers had been killed or captured. He welcomed this rag-tag company, especially the enthusiasm of his new officer. He seemed to have a better understanding of the need to fight using the land rather than set piece engagements with troops in line abreast marching boldly into the enemy's canon, especially now that Puno had been occupied. There had been little contact with Chilean forces and the small outpost of Peruvians had little to do but patrol the northern part of the Lake and live as best they could. Here the two men came to appreciate each other despite their differences in social class and rank. The patrician officer from the city learnt how the professional soldier Garcia carried on his trade with a strong but friendly leadership. Garcia on his part, who had a natural suspicion of all the officer classes, saw that this Comandante was prepared to learn the new arts of war and truly cared for his men. There was also a common bond between the mountain upbringing of the soldier and his officer. Garcia was surprised that this man, with an education far above his own and with a wider knowledge of the world of anyone that he had known, could speak fluent Quechua[8] and knew the customs of the people of the mountains. When offered a hot cup of mate de coca[9] on a cold winter's night, Garcia was surprised when his officer poured a little onto the ground as an offering to Pachamama, the Incan earthmother.

[8] Pronounced "ketch-uwah" is the language of the Incas and many other peoples of the Andes. Called the Runa Simi in their language, it was originally not a written language and is more accurately a group of languages spoken differently in many places.
[9] An excellent traditional herbal tea still used today and made from the coca bush. It is very useful for altitude sickness.

So the two men became friends; although neither would admit to such a relationship between a Comandante and Sargento. On October 20, 1883 hostilities between Chile and Peru formally came to an end under the Treaty of Ancón and the small company marched the long road back to Cuzco. Here as a reward for his "gallant action", Moreno was promoted to Teniente Coronel and made the Exploration Officer of his Battalion. Moreno was under no illusions about this. The Exploration Officer had the task of exploring enemy territory to gather firsthand information noting their disposition and strength; in other words his work became the forerunner of today's military intelligence. In uncharted territory it was his task to also draw the charts, often alone, but he was given a good horse and considerable freedom of movement. For the Battalion this was a way of removing the troublesome officer who now had sufficient rank and political connections through his late father's friends, to make real trouble for the Junta[10] now in power. For Moreno, this was ideal. He had his independence and freedom to roam his beloved mountains and meet their people whilst contributing to his country's safety. He was greatly pleased when Sargento Garcia was attached to his position as his aide. Whether or not this arrangement was made so that there would be a stabilizing regular solder able to keep an eye on this officer or some connivance on the part of Garcia to join his friend is a matter of conjecture.

[10] Pronounced "hoonta" literally means "union" and is a governing body which runs a government. Often instituted by force, it may be a controlling body behind a government.

So now to the stories of these two men which began a few years after the War of the Pacific.

Garcia had returned to his regiment and continued with his duties. Moreno who had married many years before the War had a family and became a Senior Lecturer at his university in Cuzco. He had settled down to the daily life as an academic. Once a week he would report to his Battalion and sort out the administration tasks of his office now supervised by Garcia who had also married and settled in the city. Occasionally they would ride out into the hills on the pretext of surveying potential military routes or to visit the various outposts of lonely soldiers stationed in the hills. In fact it was relaxation for both to get away from their daily lives.

Unfortunately it is the way of the Human condition that politicians create wars, the common people must endure them and soldiers must end them with their toil and blood. A few years after settling into peace, Peru was again threated by a border dispute. This time it came from the north with Ecuador claiming territory in the foothills of Peruvian Amazonia well to the north of Cuzco, below the high peaks of the Andes and into the steamy jungles of the Amazon Basin.

Once again called up for full time duty, Coronel Moreno and his aid Sargento Garcia were attached to the Región Militar del Norte[11] that was charged with locating the enemy and his encroachment into Peruvian territory. Accompanying a small reconnaissance patrol, having left

[11] Northern Military Region.

their horses at an outpost near Aramango, the two walked north with the patrol's Cabo[12] and ten men. It was a matter of bad luck that they stumbled upon a large company of Ecuadorian regulars who had established a base well inside the border. Retreating to a rocky hill backing onto a cliff overlooking the Marañón River[13] while putting up a good defence for several days, the unit was finally overrun with Moreno and Garcia being captured.

This is the prelude to the letters which came from their prison, the old fortified hacienda of San Rafael on the Rio Pataza in the foothills east of the township of

[12] Corporal.
[13] ["MaranYON"] The main tributary of the Amazon River rising in the Andes of Peru.

Baños de Agua Santa[14]. Here in this backwater of the Ecuadorian army, Garcia found that several of the conscripts in this supply depot cum prison were related to his people not far across the border. With no love for the ruling Junta in Quito (the capital of Ecuador), it was no trouble to smuggle out the letters of Don Hernán using the traditional trade route across the border.

Not all of the letters of Don Hernán, - for it was he alone who was their author - have been used in this compilation. Many of them relate to family matters and these letters and parts of those include them have been omitted. It is only those letters which are written as stories told at San Rafael which are

[14] ["BanYOS deh Ahgwa Santa"] Bath of the Sacred Waters – a large town in the Andes of Ecuador.

included here. These have been given mainly as a record of the people and places worth remembering and written by Don Hernán out a desire to commit thought to paper before they are lost with the people who tell them.

I am indebted to the Universidad Nacional de San Antonio Abad at Cuzco where the diaries and letters of Don Hernán Moreno were accepted from his estate those many years ago. Read then the letters from San Rafael, and in reading these diverse stores told between two men learn of their character, hopes, dreams and fears and of their times in a period of transition in the rich history of the people of the Andes.

Dr. Peter T. Scott
Cuzco 2017

MAR CARIBE
COLOMBIA
Quit   Quito
MAP 2
ECUADOR
Guayaquil
Iquitos
BRAZIL
PERU
Lima
Cuzco
Andes
La Paz
BOLIVIA
Altiplano
PARAGUAY
OCEANO PACÍFICO
CHILE
Pampas
URUGUAY
Buenos Aires
Mercedes
ARGENTINA
OCÉANO ATLÁNTICO
MAP 3
Ushuaia
Tierra del Fuego
SUDAMERICA
1886
SCALE 1:35,000,000

MAPA 2
COLOMBIA
Quito
ECUADOR
Ambato
Baños
Guayaquil
Río Pastaza
Iquitos
Río Amazonas
Río Marañon
Nambale
PERU
BRAZIL
Río Ucayali
Río Urubamba
Río Madre de Dios
Lima
Cuzco
Huarcapay
Checacupe
Pucara
Puno
Juli
Copacabana
Arequipa
Lago Titicaca
La Paz
BOLIVIA
0   1000
km

MAPA 3
ARGENTINA
Estrecho de
Magallanes
CHILE
TIERRA del
FUEGO
Cabo San Diego
Ushuaia
Canal Beagle
Cabo de Hornos
0   500 km

El primera carta - el prisionero
(The first letter - the prisoner)

My dearest wife and children.

By now you would have heard that the war is over for Sargento Garcia and I, and we are now prisoners. Our little expedition into the disputed territories was a failure. We did not find the enemy; they found us! They were in larger number and quickly had us surrounded on three sides; the fourth was a sheer drop to the Rio Marañón a thousand metres below.

We fought them for three days but in the end the Northerners were too strong for us. It was good fortune, however that the good Garcia, a true Andino, found a track built by the Old People which hung on to the cliff face down to the river below. It had not been used for a very long time, for our miserable little hill had not seen habitation since the days of the Old People. At daybreak, Garcia sent those who could walk with our Cabo down the track while I stayed behind with our few wounded. Of course, the faithful Garcia disobeyed my order to leave and so he returned to stay with me.

The final attack came a few hours later; our Friends from the North liked their morning coffee so it was well after sunrise when they came. Their young Teniente[1] came running over the brow of our little hill, waving his sword and yelling encouragement to his men. This was his great moment of glory, his fear was only hidden by his desire to be a

[1] ["Teni-YEN-tay"]Lieutenant

hero. What a letdown it must have been for him!

Instead of finding a gallant force defending the hill to its last man, he found Garcia and I sitting on a pile of rocks smoking our cigars, with our forlorn group of wounded huddled around us.

"¿Imaynalla Kasanki?"[2] Garcia greeted the solders in his native Quechua, for most of them looked like Andino conscripts. They were all so confused by a greeting in the Runa Simi[3] that they stopped and looked at our little band with some puzzlement. Their Teniente had lost his bravado in finding only a handful of men defending his great

[2] [Imay-naya khai-shan-key?] "How are you?" in the Quechua language.
[3] ["Roona Seemi"] Literally " the people's language" is the name given by speakers of Quechua to their own language .

objective, commanded only by a very senior officer and one Sargento. When I stood and handed him the hilt of my sword, he could only stammer "gracias, mi Colonel" and looked at the ground like a little schoolboy confronted by his teacher.

What followed was an anticlimax. We were taken down the hill along a small, dirt track for some hours. Eventually we reached a clearing on the river flats where their army had their encampment. Garcia and I were very surprised at the extent of this encampment. It seemed to be about company strength with a well-cleared central plaza surrounded by several large tents and supply wagons. Their incursion across the border seemed to be well-planned and thorough. At one end was a larger tent raised on a small platform of logs. From this emerged the leader of this party, a thin-faced Capitán[4] who did not look pleased to see us.

"Well! Who are you?" He asked with a brusque voice and a sneer, "a Colonel, no less! What are you doing in our territory?" He took my sword from the Teniente who had stood a respectful distance from me and his superior, and threw it contemptuously into his tent.

I ignored his questions and asked that my wounded be cared for. Such a man as this did not require an answer. The Capitán, whose name I later learnt was Moralez and a career soldier, with a tough reputation – well at least according to his men who had no love for his style of leadership – turned to his junior officer

4 ["Capi-TAAN"] Captain.

and instructed him to take me to another tent across the clearing. Garcia was led away towards our wounded who lay in a pitiful state upon the ground. None of the soldiers who had noticed our arrival had made any attempt to assist them.

After a brief and brusque interrogation which had yielded little except my name and regiment, the Capitán left the tent. Through the opening I saw him speak to a Sargento who mounted his horse and galloped out of the clearing. No doubt he was sent to report our capture. Two soldiers entered the tent and motioned me out. I was taken across the clearing where Garcia and our wounded were being guarded. It had begun to rain as it often did in the late afternoon on this side of the Andes. Soon there were large puddles on the bare ground, the huge drops made expanding circles in them as they fell. Our three wounded men tried in vain to shelter below the tree under which they had been placed but it gave scant protection. Garcia tried to make them as comfortable as possible but his cloak had been taken by the soldiers so I gave him mine with which to give them some shelter.

Soon we were loaded onto a wagon which contained many empty sacks. Garcia and I were bound hand and foot much to the laughter of our captors who spoke a tongue which I recognised as one of the Amazonian dialects. Two soldiers, shorter and stockier than the rest climbed onto the front seat and started the mules on our journey.

The rain had passed now but the wagon was becoming more and more uncomfortable. Our wounded suffered with every lurch of the wagon. Garcia and I could do little for them. After a few hours on the rough track which ran north parallel to the hilly country on our right, the wagon stopped. Our drivers unhitched the two mules leading them to a patch of grass where they shackled their legs. The tailboard of the wagon was dropped. With looks of both shame and despair our two drivers carefully carried our wounded off the wagon and placed them onto some dry bags which they had placed under the wagon.

"Please forgive us, Señor Colonel. We are not of that despicable company. They are Jivaro[5] and have no feelings for anyone," the older of the two men said in a low

5 One of the indigenous peoples of the headwaters of the Marañon River and its tributaries, in northern Peru and eastern Ecuador. They had a fearsome reputation as head hunters.

voice. "We belong to the supply depot and come from the mountains".

"Agradiseyki,"[6] Garcia replied. This brought a smile to the man's lips for he knew that Garcia, who was a little taller than most of his people, was also an Andino like himself.

Reverting to Spanish for my benefit, because they assumed that an officer of Spanish blood would not speak the language of the common people of the mountains, the younger man whose name was Luis, apologised for our treatment and removed the ropes from our hands and legs.

6. [ahgray-de-see-key] An expression loosely translated from the Quechua as "Thank you very much".

"Please, Señor Colonel, do not try to escape. We will do our best for you and your men. Besides, there is nowhere to go here, especially with your wounded. Will you give me your word that you will not try to escape?"

I gave him my parole[7] as the track along which we had come only led back to our enemy's camp and the road ahead was towards an unknown destination deeper into Ecuador. Garcia and I sat under the wagon with our three wounded men. They felt a lot better on the sacks which had been spread upon the ground. Soon our two guards managed to light a fire from dry tree bark and brought us some hot coffee. It was bitter but most

---

[7] Parole is a temporary release of a prisoner who verbally agrees to certain conditions including not escaping. From the French for "voice".

welcome. Perhaps our fortunes had begun to improve.

It was a slow and very rough trip. Garcia and I looked after our wounded the best we could. It took three days along a road which followed the base of the mountains which began to grow in size as we headed further north. Eventually we began to climb into the hills moving now towards the west as the forest gave way to bare hillsides of grass and low shrubs. We were now following a narrow mountain stream which the drivers called the Rio Pastaza, a tributary of the Marañón which itself eventually flowed into the Amazon much further to the east. It was late afternoon, the sun had disappeared below the mountains giving the sky a yellow glow. The temperature had dropped markedly, carefully Garcia covered our men with more of the sacks. The track had also widened and now was a reasonable mountain road which dropped off to our right into the gorge through which the Rio Pastaza flowed.

"We will be there soon, Señor Colonel." Luis said. "Forgive me but I will have to tie you both up again. You know…it would not look good to our Comandante."

So we were again bound but with less zeal than our captor in the jungle. Not long afterwards we rounded a tight bend to arrive at an old hacienda on a high cliff overlooking the river. It is very secure, of course, being on a high cliff with the river far below on one side, and steep hills on the other side of the narrow valley. Luis explained that the estate is called San Rafael[8], which perhaps is a good sign, for the Saint may aid in our recovery from being captured.

It is a solid building which we were told was built by the Spanish in the days when attack from the Puruhuaes[9] was a real threat. It had few external windows making it an ideal prison. Its overall appearance was one of neglect as it had been obviously derelict for some time. Luis explained - apologised really - that it had been commandeered by the military just a few months ago to become a supply depot in support of their expansion into the Amazon Basin.

8. Saint Raphael is an Archangel and the patron saint of travellers and nurses
9. [Pooru-waes] The indigenous people living in this region

The two huge studded doors opened to allow Luis to drive the wagon through the large archway into the outer courtyard. Here we were greeted by a small group of people who showed both curiosity and compassion for the forlorn occupants of the wagon. An officer pushed his way through the throng. This was the Comandante who commanded the depot.

After a quick look into the wagon he turned to his people and began to issue orders in a load, firm voice.

"Jose, Roberto, Joaquín, Santiago, take these poor men to the main room, prepare beds and a good fire." He ordered. "Maria, Antonia, Florencia, prepare food - a good hot soup and bread. Rodrigo take my best horse and ride to the city to fetch Doctor Ernesto. Tell him that it is an emergency."

Turning to me as I wearily attempted to sit on the rear of the wagon "Oh mi Colonel! Please forgive the treatment you have received at the hands of my countrymen. Luis, how could you tie these men and treat them like animals trussed for the market?" Luis gave me a weak smile and raised eyebrows as if to say 'that is the way of life'.

The Comandante took a knife from one of his men and quickly cut the ropes binding me and then those of Garcia and the wounded. "Colonel - and you too, Sargente - please come into the main room. Sit by the fire and rest. Food will be here soon then we shall see about beds and some new clothes."

The group of people quickly disperse into organised groups who knew what the Comandante wanted. We were led through another archway and then into a large room which separated the austere outer courtyard from the inner courtyard. There was a large fire burning in the hearth. The nights in these mountains were beginning to get cold, and a bitter wind was blowing down the valley from the higher slopes.

"Forgive me, Colonel. Permit me to name myself as Antonio Castillo Andrés, the Commanding Officer of this small supply depot." The Comandante spoke with a strong but gentle voice. It was now, for the first time that I could observe our new captor. He was a man of some age. Perhaps well over his sixtieth year but he carried his tall frame well and his grey hair and beard were still strong. It was obvious that here was a professional soldier of great experience and breeding. The armless sleeve of his immaculate jacket was pinned across his breast and above it several rows of medals and campaign ribbons. Later I was to learn that he was a veteran of some distinction in the war with my country in 1858 and of the civil war in Ecuador in 1859. He had lost his arm at an engagement at Guayaquil, the main port city of Ecuador, whilst leading his company against opposing forces in the civil war. Since then he had been given administrative tasks, and now this was his last command at San Rafael as Supply Officer for the Eastern Campaign. An efficient and humane officer, he was loved by all of his men at the hacienda. Some had served with him in the past, but for the most part his men now comprised old soldiers and young, local conscripts.

Several of the older men had their wives and families at the hacienda; the woman folk acting as domestics. The depot therefore was more of a well-organised family than a strict military establishment with Don Antonio as the beloved head of the family. Of course, there were also the trappings of an efficient military unit there; always ready to present a martial face to anyone visiting from outside, but generally the soldiers went about their daily tasks with little of the protocol and polish of a larger city military establishment. Our arrival then, expected, thanks to our tough Capitan's horseman, was a matter for the ministrations of the family rather than the receipt of prisoners.

Now, after our hardships of the previous few days I am comfortable and being treated well. The room given to me is large, with good furnishings, there is even a small balcony overlooking the river far below. Sargento Garcia has been allowed to stay with me as my servant, but I cannot really imagine that solid professional soldier in such a role. Never-the-less, he attends me each day as well as bringing me news from outside. He has a small room in the lower regions of the house but, like the rest of the hacienda, it is well guarded. Many of our guards are indeed conscripts, largely untrained and fresh from the farm, but they share a common heritage with Garcia's people who speak the same language.

Luis, our original driver holds some sway in the hacienda even though he is only a common soldier. This is his peoples' traditional land where he has many relatives in the nearby city of

Baños de Agua Santa. He has relatives who were trading salt from here in the mountains to people in the lowlands of what is now Peru from before the invasion of the Incas and then the Spaniards. The subsequent Spanish, wars of independence and then the arbitrary drawing of the border between our two counties had not stopped this trade. Now of course it is called smuggling unless you pay the appropriate government taxes, but Luis' people do not. Then, who worries about this? The customs agents on this side of the border are also related to Luis! This is how this letter has reached you, my darling. Across the border with the mule pack train and then into the normal postal service of Peru. Unfortunately this can only be a one-way communication and I beg you not to disclose it in fear that our good Luis will be found out.

However, please tell my superiors that Garcia and I are well and that our two men Soldado de Primera[10] Pedro Álvares Muñoz and Soldado[11] Enrique Ernesto Garrido Marín are receiving medical care in the village hospital. Please stress that my superiors should make only the usual enquiries to the Ecuadorean government as to our existence. The reply to those enquiries should make good reading for I am sure that the military Junta which controls their puppet government will deny all knowledge of our capture. Perhaps soon an opportunity for some exchange may occur and the Junta will suddenly be made aware of our existence as 'recovering guests' in their country

[10] Lance Corporal
[11] 'Soldier' – better translated to 'Private'

and will repatriate us all with great apologies.

I must go now, my love. Tomorrow is another day.

El segunda carta - el abuelo
(The second letter - the grandfather)

I am sorry that there has been some time since my last letter. There has not been an appropriate opportunity for it to be passed on until now. Life in our prison has become routine now and Don Antonio, the Comandante has been a generous host despite his sudden and unexpected role as our jailer.

It is cold, even for April, and the wind is howling down the valley off the snow of Volcan Tungurahua[1] not far from the town. Today is the feast day of San

1. ["tungu-agu-wah"] From Quechua *tunguri* [throat] and *rahua* [fire] or "throat of fire" is an active volcano above the town of Baños de Agua Santa.

Jorge[2], the patron saint of soldiers, so the Comandante has gone to his Headquarters in the city of San Juan de Ambato only some twenty kilometres over the mountain for the celebration. Naturally our guards are celebrating too, although I am not sure whether it is for the Saint's day or the Comandante's absence! Garcia, a good friend to all, has obtained a jug of chicha[3] and has been allowed to visit me for a few hours – probably so our guards can celebrate without the responsibility of watching us.

We were seated on my little balcony and watching the storm clouds coming down

2. [Pronounced "Horhey"] Spanish for St. George, whose feast day is April 23rd.
3. ["chee-chah"] A traditional Andean fermented beer made from maize.

the valley. There was lightning in that storm, with the thunder reverberating off the valley wall in front of us. The air was very still around us weighing heavily on our souls. Garcia took a long swig of his beer then threw the remains in his cup over the parapet to the earth below in respect for Pachamama[4] as was our custom.

"You know Patrón[5]" he said with a low serious tone to his voice," it was not luck that helped me to find that track off that accursed hill."

4. ["PAH-cha-ma-ma"] Pachamama is the earth goddess revered by the indigenous people of the Andes. She is a fertility goddess responsible for the harvest and earthquakes. Even today it is considered good manners to spill a little of one's drink onto the ground in her honour.
5. Patron or more colloquially "Boss" – a mark of respect.

I looked at him and saw that his face was very grave with a worried, almost frighten look about it. Garcia had been my Sargento and friend for many years even though we both would not admit to the latter because of the difference in our rank. He was a brave, professional soldier who was usually happy and full of confidence. I had never seen that expression before.

"Why do you say that, Garcia?" I asked.

He looked up at me and said "It is a difficult story, Patrón. One which I have never told before. May I be permitted to tell it to you now? It would be of much help to me."

I filled his cup and he told me his story.

"I swear that this is true, mi Colonel" and with that he crossed himself and poured a little beer over the parapet to the bare rocks below.

"I was just a young soldier, you understand. I had just been made Cabo and was on a patrol with our young Teniente into that green hell to our east they call Amazonia. It was yet another problem between the Jivaros and the settlers, but there was some doubt as to who was our real enemy. The jungle along the Rio Marañón is unforgiving and kills any outsider who ventures into its territory. Have you been into the jungle, Patrón?"

"Yes, Garcia, I replied. As a young man I went down the Rio Madre de Dios[6] which is well to our southeast and east of Cuzco, but it was relatively tame then, as the missionaries had been there for many years. The Campa[7] people who lived there generally did not like us Blancos[8] and would occasionally make trouble."

"That is true, Patrón. That place is also part of my story, so you will know what I mean when I tell it," he replied.

He took another mouthful of beer and looked down at his feet. "Our young Teniente was very new at being a soldier.

6. A river in the southern part of Peruvian Amazonia which runs northeast into the Amazon River.
7. An indigenous tribe in that part of Peruvian Amazona, the Asháninca ["Ashani-BAH"] - known to the Incas as the Campa.
8. Literally means "whites" and could be used as a derogatory racial term

He had come from a famous family of soldiers but truly I did not feel that he had much confidence in himself, especially not where we were going. We had come down from the mountains from our Company Headquarters at Jaén de Bracamoros[9] and cut our way through the jungle for several days until we reached the Rio Marañón flowing east into the mighty Rio Amazon. It was very difficult, as the river cuts through many gorges and where it is less steep, most of its banks are slippery mud covered in jungle. We lost one of our Cabos, Diego Torres to a deadly fer-de-lance[10] and then Sargento Balleña was taken by a caiman[11]

9. Or more simply called Jaén is a town in the northern part of Peru named after a town in Spain and the Bracamoros [from the Quechua for "painted face"] the local inhabitants.
10. Literally "spearhead" and is a large and venomous snake.
11. A South American alligator.

when we were crossing a river. All of the time the insects -the mosquitos and gnats – and other nameless horrors were biting us and keeping us awake at night. By the time we had finally reached our objective, which was a small hill near the junction of the Rio Santiago, we were in a bad way. Our young Teniente was now very afraid, he was lost now without the guidance of our lost Sargento Balleña. To make things worse, our native scouts had left us saying that the Jivaro were all around and after our blood."

Garcia stood up and looked down the valley into the rain which was approaching from the mountains beyond. He turned towards me to continue his story.

"It was raining there too, Patrón, like it always does in the jungle when darkness falls. I was with the Teniente under a shelter which I had made from my cape and was trying to get a small fire going to make him some coffee. Suddenly he looked up over my shoulder, and loudly exclaimed 'Abuelo!'[12]

His eyes were very wide and I turned and saw a most fearsome sight. There, just in the faint light of my candle, at the edge of the bushes was an old man. He was a Blanco, like you Patrón but he was only wearing shorts and sandals and his body was painted in black stripes from the juice of the huito plant[13] like the

12. Grandfather.
13. ["hwito"] or *Genipa americana* is a species of plant native to northern South America. It has many uses but the juice will stain the skin black.

Campas do. His lower face was painted blue up past the eyes and his forehead was painted yellow. On this was painted a black snake. Now as you know, I have never been afraid of much mi Colonel, but that night my hair stood on end and I shivered in fear.

'Do not be afraid, mi Nieto[14].' The old man said, 'for I have come to take you and your men home. There is an old trail nearby which the Old Ones made when they came down from the mountains to trade salt for quri– what you would call gold - the sweat of Inti, the god of the Sun. It is an old trail but I know it and the Jivaro will not follow me for they are afraid.'

14. Grandson.

"Now Patrón," Garcia continued, "I finally understood who this man was. I had heard the stories from the veterans about the wars with the Campas many years ago. There had been a famous leader of our patrols, who was the abuelo of our very own officer. This man, you understand, had grown up on the Madre de Dios, where you yourself have travelled. It was a very wild place then, but this man had lived with his family on their plantation and had grown up with the boys of the local people. He learned everything there was about the jungle and its wild inhabitants. In time, this man became friends with an old brujo[15] who adopted him as his son and initiated

15. ["Broo-HO"] A shaman or traditional medicine man. Often belonging to secret clans.

him into his Anaconda Clan – that was the snake sign on his forehead.

When hostilities broke out with the Jivaro, further to the north, this man joined the army and became a scout. The Jivaro soon learned to be afraid of this man. He was a brujo who could move quickly and unseen through the jungle. They called him Chullachaqui[16] – the Jungle Spirit, and he was death to them".

I listened to this story with much interest. Garcia had a very serious and intense expression on his face.

16. ["coola-KHAR–tee"] The Spanish form of the Quechua form Chullachaki meaning uneven-footed - is a malignant jungle spirit. Some myths describe it as an old man, others say that it is the embodiment of the jungle itself which pervades every living thing.

"Patrón, you need to know what this word 'Chullachaqui' means, for it will show you the power of this man. Chullachaqui is not a spirit living in the jungle, for there are many of these; it is the very spirit and life of the jungle itself. It can be a very good spirit for those who know and practice its ways, but for a puningare[17], or a stranger like ourselves, it is a very bad spirit which is with you all the time you are in his land. Did you not feel him when you were on the Madres de Dios, Patrón?"

I had been listening intently to Garcia's gripping story and was taken back momentarily by his question.

17. ["Poonin-GAH-reey"] Campa term for a stranger, a gringo!

"Yes, Garcia," I replied. "I do believe I know what you mean. Especially at night when the darkness closes in and it is only the light from the fire which keeps it at bay. It gives one a strong feeling of depression and foreboding. I never felt very happy at night in the jungle".

Garcia nodded his head in agreement with my feeling and continued his story. "The old man told his grandson to get ready – 'we will go soon whilst the rain was still falling. Every man was to go, and litters were to be made for those who could not walk'. This man will come behind me and make a trail for you to follow' the old Brujo said, pointing to me. I was afraid, but stood and nodded that I would do as he asked.

So, with a new vigour and a fire in his
eyes which I had never seen before, my
young Teniente gathered the remains of
our patrol and I followed the old man
into the darkness of the jungle. It seemed
like many hours before the sun sent its
feeble grey light through the trees, but
we were going away from this hell, so
time did not matter. The Jivaros did not
come near as they were afraid of
Chullachaqui so we made good progress.
We walked like this for several days, the
old man leading at a fast pace and in the
closeness of the jungle I had great
difficulty in keeping him in sight.

Once, when we had reached the open
forest on the foothills of our beloved
mountains, he turned and looked at me.
His stare was intense but a smile came on

his painted face. 'You are a good man. You have looked after my Nieto so I will watch over you also.'

I thought at the time that this was a strange thing to say, but I put the thought aside and continued to follow him along the unseen trail. Eventually we climbed up out of the forest and along a well-defined trail and into our familiar mountains. The men were happy now, because they were all true Andinos who could breathe clean air again.

A day later, we were on the ridge overlooking our little village of Jaén. The old man gave his grandson one last embrace, and with a wave of his hand, walked off back to his forest.

So we arrived back at our Company stockade and were greeted by our friends who had given us up for dead. After we had made our reports and restored our bodies and souls, I made some coffee and took it to the young Teniente. I found him alone in his small room, sitting on his bed. He held a letter in his hand and tears were flowing freely.

Now mi Colonel, I had seen this young officer change in the past few days from a frightened young man into a leader of men. Why did he have cause to cry?

What is wrong, Teniente?' I asked. He handed me his letter but I said Teniente, I am sorry, but I cannot read.

He took the letter from my hand and looked up into my face with tears still in his eye. 'It is from my mother, Garcia' he said. 'In it she tells me that her father, my grandfather, the man they called Chullachaqui, quietly passed away at his home in Iquitos[18]. Before he died she asked him to watch over me, her only son. She said that he smiled, closed his eyes and departed this world in peace'.

With an uncertain look he continued. 'Cabo Garcia, this letter arrived here only one day after we had started our patrol into the jungle.'

Garcia looked at me intently as though he wished to show the importance of his

18. Iquitos – a large city in the north of the Peruvian Amazonia

story. "So you see, Patrón. It was not good fortune that led me to find that trail which saved you and I and our men, but the old abuelo."

El tercera carta - la salvación de Baños
(The third letter – the salvation of Baños)

We had now settled into a comfortable routine at San Rafael. About seven in the morning, give or take some minutes as time was not of an importance here, there would be a knock on my door, it would be unlocked and Ambrosio, the Comandante's general factotum would enter. Like many of the staff here, he is an old soldier devoted to his officer and of a friendly disposition.

"Buenos dias, Senior Colonel." He would always say and he would have a hot cup of coffee in one hand and a jug of hot water for my morning ablutions in the other. He would place the jug on the dresser and the cup on my bedside table.

I would thank him and he would bow and leave, closing the unlocked door behind him. As I had given my parole not to escape for both Garcia and myself, we were both allowed to roam freely about the hacienda. Of course the outer doors were locked and a guard, often asleep, was at the front entrance; more to warn of any approaching official than to keep the two prisoners inside.

After washing and shaving, I would dress ready for breakfast at eight. This was a punctual time as Comandante Castillo demanded it. My uniform had been thoroughly cleaned and pressed just after our arrival, but both Garcia and I had been given new sets of clothing. There is no shortage of necessary items within a supply depot. What they do not have they can requisition with such authority that the items usually arrived. The Comandante's reputation within the lower echelons of the military and the priority given to the Amazon expansion ensured a prompt response to any request.

Breakfast was taken in the main hall at long table occupied only by Comandante Castillo and myself. Garcia, as was befitting his rank in this formal setting, ate with the other men in a room next to the kitchen. Coffee and an assortment of bread and pastries with jam and cheese were served and sometimes Ambrosio would ask if we would like an egg. This was usually lightly fried on one side and served separately on a small plate.

Conversation would usually be minimal although Don Antonio always acted as a good host and would enquire after my health and apologise for my situation and the lack of entertainment. The Comandante had a good supply of old books and was very generous with his wine, spirits and cigars, all of which were of the best quality.

Wiping his chin with his napkin as a sign that he had finished his meal, the Comandante looked up and smiled.

"It will be a fine day, today Colonel Moreno. Would you care to ride with me into the town and see some more of our fine country? Perhaps it will not be as exciting as your most recent visit to our jungles but certainly of some interest never-the-less"

Comandante Castillo provided me with a fine horse from his small stable and so we rode out through the gates of the hacienda at a very leisurely pace. The road was merely a cart-track which followed the flat, narrow bank of the steep-sided river valley. The hills rose up very high on either side of the valley and unlike those on the western side of the Andes, these slopes were green with lush vegetation. Here and there, where the slope was not severe, some of the natural vegetation had been cleared for small cultivation of crops giving the slopes a patchwork of greens in different textures. To my eye, these crops seem to be hanging onto these slopes with a tenacity only rivalled by the narrow tracks which led up to them.

The Comandante explained that our journey at this leisurely pace would take about three hours; a good time for a discussion away from the life of the hacienda. Mostly we spoke of our personal lives; our homes, our families and of the futility of wars in which our governments seem to entangle themselves.

"You will like our little town of Baños," the Comandante said. "It has an interesting history and is one of the places of spiritual significance in our country. Would you like to hear its story?"

"Certainly, Señor," I replied for I knew that Comandante Castillo was both a well-educated man and a good raconteur. So this is the Comandante's story:

"Baños was founded by the Dominicans[1] who set up a small friary in the region around 1570. Of course it had been populated for many years by the Puruhuaes, the local people, who themselves had been assimilated into the Incan Empire in the fifteenth century. No doubt both peoples were attracted to these valleys by the hot springs from the volcano and the fertile soil. For the Incas, this was also a gateway to the Amazon Basin further east as it still is today. The

[1] The Order of Preachers (Latin: *Ordo Praedicatorum*, O.P.), known as the Dominican Order, is a traveling order of the Roman Catholic Church founded by the Spanish priest Dominic of Caleruega in France in 1216.

Inca nobility also like to come here for bathing in the hot waters which are very beneficial to the health. In the local language of the Puruhuaes they refer to this as 'ishpaypae' – bathing in the urine of Mama Tungurahua – which I do not think was a disrespectful term and is probably best translated in meaning to 'waters'. Certainly the waters seem to have a therapeutic value.

So the Dominicans came and set up their little congregation to bring the word of God to the Heathen. Of course the local people and their Incan overlords had their own complex religion with Inti the Sun and Pachamama the earth goddess being most important in their theology. Even today, the people still give offerings to the old deities – just in case - you understand.

One old story recounts how the Sacristan[2] of their church was visited by an image of the Virgin Mary who told him that they should build a shrine near one of the many hot springs which occur in the district and that this would be a place of curing and salvation for lepers and others with sickness. So today, in our little stone church we have the statue of Our Lady of the Rosary of Agua Santa de Baños, and our town is a place of pilgrimage from all over the country."

"It makes for a good story, Señor," I commented. "There are many places in my country and in Europe which have special shrines to the Virgin and many of the saints. It builds on the faith of the

[2] An official of a church charged with caring for the vessels and other accoutrements of the church

common people and of course is good revenue for the Church."

"Ah. You are too cynical, Colonel." The Comandante replied. "Many have been cured by these waters. Whether it is by their faith or by the miracles promised by the Virgin, it is beyond the comprehension of a simple soldier like me.

But there is another legend which concerns the faith of the people of Baños which perhaps is a lot more dramatic as it concerns our volcano. Wait and in a few moments when we go around the next corner you will see Mama Tungurahua."

Indeed, as we came around the corner of a steep ridge running down to the river below, I saw at the end of the long, steep-sided valley to our left, the magnificent shape of the volcano Tungurahua.

It had the typical cone shape of Andean volcanoes, similar to others which I had seen in Peru. I found that the Comandante shared my fascination with these giants. Now, sleeping in the distance it still commanded some degree of awe and inspiration. Its lower slopes were vegetated for the most part except where they had been eroded by landslides. A deep ravine cut into the slope facing us. The summit, now flat and broken by its crater's edge after many eruptions and erosion, was swathed in small white clouds. I had been in one small eruption well to the south in Peru, which had been at a distance but it was still a terrifying experience. The rapidity of the vertical ejection of a very large cloud of grey ash had been almost unbelievable. The enormous roar of its sound was enhanced by the thunder claps of the lightning which was generated by such a sudden movement of hot gas and ash. Once the huge mushroom cloud had reached its great height it spread out on the high altitude winds and then fell like hot sand upon all in its path. I had felt a little of this hot rain and had not waited to be overcome. I had spurred my horse to a gallop in a safe direction. And this was considered only a small eruption in an unpopulated region!

The Comandante continued his story:

"I think that it was in 1773 when the volcano had a massive eruption or so the Dominican scholar Don Emiliano de

Velasco recorded. His description was most horrendous. After days of multiple earth tremors the volcano belched forth a prodigious amount of ash and heavier material in a great explosion. Luckily most of the fine ash was pushed away from Baños by the prevailing winds. This was not good for those in the village on the side of the volcano that was totally destroyed by the ash fall which collapsed buildings and poisoned all of the livestock.

In Baños the population was in a great state of panic but then as the great cloud collapsed, lava and fiery clouds of ash flowed towards the village over the side of the volcano down the deep ravine which you can still see on the this side of the volcano. This is the Quebrada Bascún[3] through which a river still runs, right through the western part of the town and into the Rio Pastaza.

Seeing the lava approaching their town, some people ran to the church and brought out the statue of the Virgin de Agua Santa and carried her outside into the plaza, praying to her for salvation. It is said that someone saw the statue raise its hand and with that the lava stopped at the edge of the town. Another story of the faithful, I suppose, but it is still a good story and I believe that the townspeople plan to rebuild the small stone church as a great basilica for the veneration of our protector, the Virgin de Agua Santa."

[3] Bascun ravine cut by the river of that name.

It was an interesting story, one which showed the faith of this toughened soldier. I have seen many miracles in my lifetime which I cannot explain; mostly the heroic actions of men in difficult situations so I could not comment on the Comandante's assessment of the people of Baños. We rode on in silence for a while.

Suddenly the Comandante struck his forehead with the palm of his hand. "Stupido!" he exclaimed. "Today is Wednesday. How could I forget! I had hoped to have you meet Fray[4] Dominic at the church. He acts as our padre at the hacienda, but on Wednesdays he goes out to the outlying farms on his mule and gives alms and his blessings to the poor.

[4] "Fray" is the Spanish honourific for "friar"

Sometimes he also gives advice which is often more practical than religious and the people hereabouts love him as Padre Dom."

The Comandante looked up to the sky and gave a loud sigh. "Oh well. Never mind. I am sure that you will meet him soon enough."

We rode the short distance remaining down into the steep bank of the Pastaza and up into the town. Here I found streets which were well-paved with cobbles from the stream and small houses made of mud-brick, often limed on the outside and painted in bright colours. The people were obviously proud of their town and seemed happy to see us; many gave personal greetings to the Comandante. "Buenas tardes[5], Don Antonio" they would say with a smile; the men taking off their hats and the ladies giving a small nod of their head.

We dismounted at the town's plaza, tied the reins of our horses to a rail at its edge and walked into its centre. It was only a small square with the church and the Dominican convent with its surrounding wall on one side and single storied shops and houses on the other three. It was not like the grand Plaza de Armes[6] I have seen in other towns and cities. There was no statue to a Conquistador, Liberator or Inca; no fountain and as yet no grand

[5] "Good afternoon"
[6] Literally "Arms Square" or "Parade Ground" which represented the first site of the military stockade established by the early Spanish settlers. Many Latin American cities or towns have a square thus named. Usually it will have the main church or cathedral on one side and the government offices on the opposite side. Shops usually occupy the other two sides.

official buildings. The pathways through the plaza seem to be in a grid pattern with a variety of tall trees and palms in between.

The Comandante was very proud of this little town. "We have a new Alcalde[7]. Well…he is still a priest and a gringo from Belgium, but he has assumed the position of Alcalde and has great plans for the future of our town with the building of public works and a stone basilica in honour of our Virgin."

We lunched at a small café with coffee and locro de papa[8] and bread. We paid

[7] Mayor – In 1887 the Belgian priest Tomás Halflants assumed the position of Alcalde and built many buildings, bridges and began the construction of the Nuestra Señora de Agua Santa

[8] This is a famous Ecuadorian soup with avocados, potatoes and cheese.

our respects to the Virgin at the church then remounted before heading back east along the road to the hacienda. Along the way, Don Antonio recounted the life of his friend Fray Dominic, a man whom he admired. No doubt I would meet him soon.

El cuarta carta – el padre
(The fourth letter – the padre)

Another day had come. I had returned to my room after breakfast with the Comandante, when there was a knock at the door and Garcia entered as was his usual habit.

"Buenos dias Patrón![1]" he said with a smile on his weather-beaten face. "You must be in trouble. There is a priest asking for you downstairs."

"Thank you, Garcia. Well, for my sins we had better go and see what the good father wants of us." I replied, putting on my boots and jacket.

[1] Literally "Good Morning, Patron" but here it is best translated as "Good morning, Boss!"

We walked along the loggia[2] and down the covered stairway which led to the inner courtyard of the hacienda. Garcia diplomatically and quietly gave his farewell as he continued down the stairs to the level below that housed the kitchen where the stove and good coffee would be still hot.

Sitting on a small bench under an orange tree sat an old man with the white cassock and the shouldered black cappa[3] of a Dominican Friar. Both the man and his vestments had seen better days. The dark skin of his face and hands had been deeply tanned by years of exposure to the sun and the elements, while his scant grey hair hung in long, unkempt strands.

[2] A covered balcony, often with a colonnade which runs around the upper floor of a courtyard.
[3] The black cape and hood typical of the Dominican order

This then must be Fray Dominic of whom the Comandante had been most lavish in his praise. Don Antonio had met the Friar many years ago in Quito, the capital, when they were both younger men. He had given me a brief account of this friar's life.

As a young student coming from a privileged family and studying natural philosophy at the university, the young Dominic had found himself caught up in the revolutionary fervour which was spreading across the entire continent of South America. A volunteer in Yaguachi Battalion of the Army of General Antonio José de Sucre, he fought in the Battle of Pichincha[4] near Quito in 1822. Horrified

4 This was fought between a Patriot army under General Antonio José de Sucre against a Royalist army commanded by Field Marshal Melchor Aymerich. The defeat of the Royalist forces loyal to Spain brought about the liberation of Quito.

by the repugnance of war and the numerous casualties on the rain-covered slopes of Volcán Pichincha, the young man fled to Europe looking for his own peace and salvation. Finally after many years of travelling without finding any meaning in his life, returned to Ecuador and joined the Dominican Order.

When the old friar stood up I saw that despite being much older than Comandante Castillo, he held himself erect and advanced with a firm and steady stride.

"Mucho Gusto![5] Colonel Moreno. "His voice was both deep and strong and his smile and alert eyes suggested a younger

[5] A general form of greeting literally meaning "much pleasure" but taken to mean "It is a pleasure to meet you" although the full phrase for this would be "mucho gusto en conocerlo."

man but one with a great knowledge of the world. "Don Antonio suggested that I pay you a call and relieve you of at least some of your burden of captivity. "

"Many thanks," I replied. "Brother Dominic, I presume?"

"At your service Señor," he said. "I took the liberty of having Maria bring us some coffee. Will you not sit with me for a while? Perhaps we have much in common?"

I joined Fray Dominic on the bench below the tree. The inner courtyard seemed to be in keeping with the appearance of the old friar. Both had been well-cared for once. Now the garden and the man had both fallen into a state of untidiness. Here in the inner courtyard of the old hacienda, the trees and shrubs had grown into a wild tangle of knurled branches and knotted trunks. The once bright tiles of the paved paths had become stained and broken while the central fountain chipped and bare.

"I must confess, Brother Dominic, I have little time for organised religion." I said.

"There. You see! We have much in common." He laughed, his broad face split with a huge grin. "I have long irritated my superiors in the hierarchy of the Church and my Order. But at least the Dominicans are an outgoing brotherhood and I am able to fulfil my tasks well away from the politics of Mother Church in Quito. A simple friar in a mountain village like Baños enables me to keep out of trouble with those of my order who have aspirations of power and position. And besides….this is where we can do the most good with the people of a simple faith. Here we can be truly the servants of God and the Virgin who protects them in their beautiful but unforgiving mountains."

Maria, the wife of one of the soldiers and who performed many of the domestic duties of the hacienda, arrived with a steaming pot of coffee and some bizcochos – the soft, buttery biscuits well known in this country.

"The Comandante tells me that you are a Militia Officer and a philosopher as well. There could be some conflict here. Often the military does not like men who think too much. These men tend to question some of the stupidity of war. Your Sargento, whom I met earlier, tells me that you are a brave man but also an officer with an independent soul. One who also is happier exploring the wilderness than carousing with those social creatures who rise to great ranks in the Army but who have limited talent and care even less for the men whom they march into battle."

"Perhaps you are right, Brother Dominic" I mused. "I do enjoy the solitude of the countryside, especially in my mountains and Garcia is a most agreeable companion who always brings me down to reality when I think too much".

The old Brother gave an impish grin to that remark and said "Do you not see God in your mountains, Colonel? Uncomplicated people like Garcia see God in everything and everywhere. Although sometimes, with the people in my mountains I wonder whether or not they still think of the gods of the old religion as well as the one true God - but to me that is of little consequence; although my superiors would not share in my opinion. My people are still faithful to Mother Church in Rome, but that is far away and the many difficulties of their daily struggles here in these mountains often need every bit of help that they can get. After all, did not the Franciscans in your country often build their churches facing the sacred mountain of the local people so that they could worship Christ as well as the Apu[6] of the mountain for protection? And do not the people welcome Inti[7] each morning when he rises in the east over

[6] Means "Lord" in Qechua. The Inca religion uses the term Apu to refer to a mountain that has a spirit that is alive and protects the local village.
[7] The ancient god of the Sun in the Incan religion and the national patron of the Inca state.

the winter snows of their sacred mountain?"

"That is true, Brother Dominic." I replied. My mother's family were in the mountains well before the Spaniards brought the Cross to this land. And I do confess that it is still a custom at home to pour a little of one's drink on the ground to show respect to Pachamama. But then I am a philosopher who thinks too much but knows so very little even though I have spent much of my life learning about what others have thought. I have learnt that good philosophers, like many good priests, realise that the more they learn, the more they see that they know very little. Logic does not often agree with faith but true knowledge tells us when logic finishes and faith begins."

"Ah! You are a philosopher indeed!" replied the friar. "But you have not told me whether or not you have seen God in your mountains as these simple people do?"

"That is true, Brother Dominic," I replied. "For all my aspirations in being a philosopher, teacher and a well-educated man, I am very ignorant in much of what people like Garcia have to teach me. They assume many things in their simple faith. They do not worry about what moves this planet around the Sun, only that it rises every morning in the east and sets in the west. The Incas kept this faith in Inti; they had no concepts of north or south, only east and west because these are were the only places which had any practical importance. As to seeing God in the mountains, or anywhere else for that matter, I sometimes think that I have wandered off God's great road to Paradise and have become lost in the dark forest created by myself and the rest of Mankind. There have been times when I have seen the hand of God both in His works of creation such as the majestic white-capped peaks of the mountains, the strength of a violent storm, the beauty of a delicate flower, but also His very soul in the hearts of people who are put to the test in heroic circumstances. Of course these visions pass too quickly and I am yet again engulfed in world of mammon."

There was something about this old friar, with his shabby appearance and his words. He was unlike my normal view of the city priests whom I had meet. These I have thought fell into two classes. The first class consists of most priests who were adequate in their administration of the sacraments and performed their priestly tasks during mass in a competent manner. They sometimes were called upon the give solace to those needing comfort but often it was inadequate with no more succour than most men or women could give to their neighbours. The other class of priests are like those men and woman within any hierarchical organisation who are conscious of their place and who are motivated by power rather from the needs of their fellows. Perhaps in my limited knowledge of the Human spirit, I have set a standard which has been too high an expectation for the usual Parish Priest and so my cynicism has made me intolerant to those who seek high office so that they may better serve the people. In my mind a priest must be a person of perfect faith, be thoroughly versed in the writings and background of the Bible and of the early saints, and above all, be a wise person who is able to teach the faith and be able to give true succour to all in need.

Perhaps I have been too hard on the religious. Here now, was a man who seemed to have the wisdom needed to be a true man of God and padre to his flock. I was to learn in our conversations over the next few months that Fray Dominic was a very learned man who had experienced much in his travels and of his contact with many others much wiser than I.

The old man took his last mouthful of coffee and looked up at the sky. "Yes, my son. Life can be difficult and always full of distractions. The road which God bids us to travel is often not so straight but like the tracks within these mountains; narrow, twisting and always difficult to perceive. We are guided by our Lord Jesus and try to do the best we can. Some follow the wisdom of other prophets and some believe that the road is theirs to make without any divine assistance. Perhaps our road has been built just for us and what is ordained is ordained. 'Insha'Allah' our Muslim brothers say. 'God willing' and submit to the will of God, for this is what 'Islam' means. Others believe that God will hear us when we pray and will change our fate. Perhaps miracles are such changes which come about when people pray for help in dire circumstances; but cynics do not believe in either miracles or God's intervention, and dismiss them as simple acts of chance. The miracles here at Baños are such examples. Did the Virgin stop the lava flow reaching the town those many years ago, or was it a simple end of a natural phenomenon? Who knows? It is a matter of faith, not logic."

He stood up and brushed the crumbs from his grey beard and almost-white habit.

"Well, my son. I must be off now. Conchita my mule is waiting to take me to those who also need me. I will say, however – and forgive me for being the padre now – that you cannot go wrong if you have faith in God, follow the Laws of Moses and the teachings of Christ. All else is the embellishment of Humankind, often for all of the wrong reasons. Do not be too hard on the simple people who have a faith stronger than yours but who still make use of the older religions, for they see many things in human nature which we, as educated men, often miss. Remember that our sins have been forgiven but sin no more. Adios, Don Hernán. ¡Hasta la vista!"[8]

With that farewell and a wave of his hand, the friar left the confines of the inner courtyard leaving me to contemplate his advice. It had been indeed a momentous visit. It is rare to meet such men and such men must be remembered.

[8] See you later.

El quinta carta – la alpaca perdida
(The fifth letter – the lost alpaca)

It was mid-morning and a beautiful day. The morning Sun threw long shadows from the colonnades as I came down the stairs which led into the wide inner courtyard. My intension was to sit in the garden and smoke an early cigar. My descent was arrested by the sound of Garcia's voice – not the harsh voice of the Primero Sargenta on the parade ground but that of Garcia the father of three children talking in a soft but animated voice. I carefully looked around the last colonnade and saw Garcia sitting under the old knurled lemon tree with a small group of the hacienda's children sitting on the grass at his feet. I knew that Garcia and his wife Constanzia had three children but I was yet to observe Garcia in this role.

Finding a small bench under the colonnades, I sat quietly where I could see the group and listened to what Garcia was saying. He was recounting a story to the children and this is what he said:

"Let me tell you, my children, of a little boy much like you, Antonio." He said, pointing to the oldest boy. "He lived in southern Peru – my country – in a valley in the mountains just north of the big lake where the Incas came from. Here his parents had a small farm."

"What is a lake, Señor Pablo?" said one of the smaller girls, whose name was Florencia like her mother.

"Well. My child" Garcia continued. "It is a very large, flat amount of water. Much bigger than the widest part of your river but not flowing like your river. It is a wide valley filled with water which takes a long while to cross if you have a boat. You can just see the high mountains on the other side. It is called 'Titicaca[1]' and it is very big. I was there with Don Hernán many years ago and we stayed with the people in the mountains."

"Did you go on a boat?" Señor Pablo?" asked Rodrigo, the son of Sargente Peña[2], the Quartermaster[3] of the hacienda.

"Ah, No, Rodrigo. We were too busy for that. But the people who live there build boats out of woven reeds from the Lake

[1] From the old name 'titiq'aq'a' given by the Aymara people who still live on its southern shores in Peru and Bolivia, meaning 'grey puma' because on a map and looking from the west it looks like a crouching puma
[2] Pronounced [pen-ya]
[3] A senior non-commissioned officer who looks after stores.

which float very well. They are Los Uros[4] and they also live in reed houses built on floating islands of reed well away from others who might harm them. But let us return to the farm in the mountains.

It is much higher there than in your mountains. Here there are trees and green plants everywhere. In his mountains, little Carlos – for that was the boy's name – there were very few trees and bushes and even those were very small. There was much grass and small shrubs and so they built their houses out of stone and adobe."

"What is adobe?" interjected Antonio the curious.

[4] The Uros people who still live on the Lake although under modern conditions with their traditional houses and customs displayed for tourists

"Mud, my little friend. Mud. The people make mud using the soil near their home and water from the river. They make a big puddle of mud. Have you not made mud puddles, Carlos?"

"Oh, si, Señor Pablo. Many times and we get very dirty and Mama scolds us and makes us have a wash in the cold river!"

"Well, the people in the mountains would also get very dirty and they too would then have to wash in the river at the end of the day. But during morning they mix straw or grass with the mud and push it into little wooden boxes which give the mud its shape. They squeeze the water out and then tip the box upside down so that the mud falls out. They then lay it out on the ground in the sun and let it dry. This is an adobe brick. They work very hard with the family all working together; the adults and all of the children too. After many days they have hundreds of bricks, so they then can build their houses."

"We build our houses out of wood" said Lucia, one of the smaller girls.

"Our house is made of stone like the hacienda" said Rodrigo with pride.

"Well there certainly are many stones in the mountains" replied Garcia. "Many people build their houses out of stone there too. Especially up in the hills where there is little soil but many stones. But to continue the story", giving Rodrigo a stern look which changed to a grin.

" The house that Carlos lived in was made of brown adobe bricks. Carlos lived with his Papa Alberto and Mama and Isadora and his brothers Santiago and Jorge and his sister little Gabriella. His abuelo[5], Don Tomás and his abuela, Doña[6] Agustina also lived with the family and it was Don Tomás and his friends who started the building many years ago.

Now listen, children. These farm houses are not like the ones around here in these narrow valleys where there is little room. Here you may have one small house. Some in the town, I am told has two heights. In Carlos' mountains where they can find some land which is flat, perhaps near a stream, they will build several small houses close together. They then connect the house with walls about as high as a man and they are also made out of adobe bricks, so that a courtyard is

[5] Grandfather
[6] Grandmother

formed. It would probably be as big as this courtyard." Garcia gestured with a sweep of his arm. "The houses would have windows and doors facing into the centre like those here in the hacienda, but their houses usually would not have an upstairs. Although in some places, farmers who are very prosperous and build their houses out of stone might build a bigger house with an upstairs room where the family live and with a space below to put their animals. However, Carlos' farm only had a house with no upstairs. They had one house with two rooms for papa and mama and the children, another house for Abuelo Tomás and Abuela Agustina and a third house for the family to cook and eat their food. There was also a small open shelter running along one wall for the animals."

"Where was the baños[7]?" cried out little Manuela with a look of concern on her little round face.

"Do not worry, my child." Garcia continued. "Outside, behind the courtyard, Abuelo Tomás had built a fine little building which contains the toilet and shelter which had a water drum and wash basin.

Now, wood was scarce in the mountains and was used only in making the two big gates for the courtyard, the frames for the rooves and the shutters for the windows – not to mention the few pieces of furniture, of course – the rooves were all made of tightly plaited straw called thatch. This made the houses very warm at night and kept out the rain, although it

[7] The word 'baños' has several meanings in Spanish. Used for the name of the nearby town, it means 'bath' like the city in England, but it could also mean 'washroom' or 'toilet'.

did not rain often in these dry mountains.

Now, can you guess what was placed on top of the rooves, children?" Garcia looked around with a broad smile and eyes wide open.

The children all looked perplexed and found an answer very difficult.

"Rocks!" spoke up Antonio, who definitely was the leader of the group because he was the eldest. "My father puts rocks on the roof so that the wind does not blow away the slabs of wood on our roof."

"Fray Dominic has a cross on his roof. He pointed to it when papa and I took some things to the church." Spoke little Lucia, her eyes wide with anticipation that her answer would be the correct one.

"Ah, very close, my child. On all of the rooves in Carlos' farm indeed have a cross but also two little bulls made out of baked clay." Garcia replied quietly.

"Two bulls!" Rodrigo exclaimed. "They would be too heavy, and why did they put bulls on the roof?"

"They are only little clay bulls, Rodrigo." Garcia said with a grin. "Very nicely painted in many colours and put onto the very top and centre part of the roof. They are called 'torita de Pucará'[8] and they, and the cross, are to there to bring good luck to all who live below the rooves."

"Now that you know about the family and their house, let us return to little

---

[8] Meaning 'little or young bulls of the town of Pucará'. A myth tells that in a great drought in Pucará, farmer took a little bull and climbed a nearby mountain hoping to sacrifice the animal to the Incan god Pacha Kamaq (Quechua "Creator of the World"). The bull resisted and his horns struck the ground from which water now flowed. Now the bulls are still placed on some rooves for good luck and fertility of the soil.

Carlos and his story, because it teaches us a very important lesson.

It had been a very good year for Papa Alberto; the maize grew high and his potato crop all came up and he had more than enough potatoes for his family to eat. Now Abuelo Tomás and Papa Alberto could make much chicha[9] and Mama Isadora and Abuela Agustina would make many lovely hot roasted potatoes.

Now because they had more potatoes than their family and friends could eat, Papa Alberto decided to preserve much of his crop by making chuño[10]. This is the way that the Ancient People would make

[9] A beer made from fermented maize.
[10] A method of freeze-drying from Quechua *ch'uñu*, meaning 'frozen potato'

their crops last a very long time – even for many years! They would take their potatoes high into the cold mountains and spread the potatoes out on the ground. At night the potatoes would freeze. The next morning in the sun the potatoes would soften and then people would tread out all of the moisture from them. They would leave them to freeze again and then tread out the moisture again. After about five days, the potatoes became black and very dry."

"Oh, but that would not taste very nice." Said little Sofia, the daughter of Maria the cook.

"You eat many potatoes here in Ecuador, do you not, little one?" Garcia replied. "I saw many potato fields on the sides of the hills when we first came here. Does not your mother cook many dishes with potatoes? Well, Mama Isadora and

Abuela Agustina would take the chuño and use it in soups, cakes from its flour and even some sweet desserts.

So one day, Papa Alberto gathered all of his llamas[11] then he and Abuelo Tomás loaded their packs with all of their extra potatoes ready to take them higher up the mountains to where they would make the chuño. Now think of how high that would be! Their farm was already twice as high as we are now and around the farm were many tall mountains so high that the snow on their tops did not melt, even during summer. It would take them several days to get to their favourite spot on the mountains and so

11 Pronounced 'lyamma' with emphases on the 'y' is a Camelid, that is a member of the family of camels which first appeared in North America about 45 million years ago and spread to South America and Asia. In the Americas they are found in in the Andes from southern Ecuador to Bolivia and include domesticated llamas and alpacas and the wild vicuñas and guanacos.

they also took other food, blankets and other things which they would need for a week in the cold mountains."

"What is a llama?" little Mariangeles, the smallest girl in the group asked.

Garcia answered softly. "In my country, up in the high mountains live the llamas. They are beautiful animals with brown or white bodies covered in soft wool, tall necks about the height of a man and we use them to carry all of our things from one place to another."

"I know all about llamas!" Rodrigo exclaimed. "Padre Dominic told me about them and showed me a drawing of one in his book. They live in the desert and are very clever."

"That is true." Garcia replied. They do like the desert. It is much too wet down here. They like to be high in the dry air.

The Ancient People took their ancestors from the desert and made them their own animals to carry their belongings. Since then my people have also done so. The llamas also have some smaller cousins; the little alpaca who has very soft wool from which we make our warm clothing and blankets and the bigger wild guanaco and their smaller relatives the vicuñas. They live in the high mountains of my country but I have not seen any up north and they would not like to live here. It is too wet.

Now…where was I? Ah, yes. Now Carlos had a little pet alpaca which he called Sumaq[12] and because Carlos had turned twelve years of age, Papa Alberto decided that he too should also come on the trip to the mountains so that he could

[12] Quechua feminine name meaning "beautiful".

learn how to make chuño and how to live in the mountains.

Papa Alberto looked at his son with a stern face and reminded him that llamas were sacred animals and that the family depended upon them to carry their potatoes to the high valleys to make chuño and to the markets. Without the llamas, the people of the high mountains would have a very difficult life. Papa Alberto had made a little bridle to put around Sumaq's neck so that Carlos could lead him along the mountain paths like Papa Alberto did with the adult llamas.

'You must never lose your little alpaca in the high mountains so keep her well protected and treat like your very own child. You must look after her all of the time and God and Urcuchillay[13] will watch over you both.' These were the words that Papa Alberto spoke to his son.

Early the next morning, just as Inti the sun came up over the mountains, Papa Alberto and Abuelo Tomás loaded their potatoes into the baskets which were carried on both sides of each llama except for the lead llama whose name was Sinchi[14]. On his back were the items needed to stay several nights; some food, warm clothing, blankets for the night chill and some sticks with which to start their fires – although there would be

13 Urcuchillay [Quechua: 'Urch-chil-AY'] was a god worshipped by Incas herders, who was believed to take the shape of a multi-coloured llama who watched over animals.
14 Quechua for "boss" or "leader"

some old vicuña dung along the trail which burns very nicely.

So off they went. Papa Alberto went first leading Sinchi by his head collar rope and the others following with their head ropes tied to the harness of the one in front. Abuelo Tomás followed in the rear with his colourful q'ipirina[15] on his back and his long walking stick with the head of the sacred puma carved at its top. Carlos and Sumaq were allowed to walk with Papa Alberto at the very front of the llama train, much to Sinchi's annoyance. Sumaq thought that she was indeed beautiful but Sinchi just put his nose in the air and gave a superior snort of disapproval. Carlos and the men wore hand-woven trousers made from alpaca

[15] Quechua term for a woven blanket tied in a triangle and carried on the back as a pack.

wool and thick ponchos[16] to keep the cold out. On their feet they wore sturdy leather ajotas[17] with tough soles for walking on the rocks. Carlos and Abuelo Tomás wore the traditional chullo[18] which were made from knitted alpaca wool but Papa Alberto also wore a sombrero on top of his chullo.

They travelled all morning across the dry valley with many stones and a few small tuffs of grass and low shrubs and up onto one of the many ridges which ran parallel to the great range of snow-capped mountains in the distance. On top of one of the ridges, which Papa called el Mirador del Cielo[19], they

---

[16] A thick, woven cape worn over the shoulders with a hole for the head
[17] Sandals which cover most of the feet, now often made from rubber.
[18] From Aymara: 'ch'ullu', these are knitted hats with earflaps. The first *chullo* that a child receives is traditionally knitted by his father
[19] Spanish: 'the lookout of the sky'

stopped for a lunch of small cakes made by Abuela Agustina and water from the waterskin tied to Sinchi's harness. They sat upon the ground where the stones had been cleared and the llamas were released to graze on the small tuffs of grass nearby. Carlos noticed that they were surrounded by many piles of tiny stones which were scattered here and there. They looked like many small towers and consisted of about five or six rounded stones piled up with the largest on the bottom and the smallest on top. Papa Alberto explained that these were apachetas[20] built by travellers as they climbed the trail. He said that as they walked the trail, they would pick up a

---

[20] From the Quechua and Aymara :word 'apachite', these small pebble towers not only acted as trail markers and campsites but some say that they were also places of the spirits called 'huacas', the stones being piled as thanks to Pachamama the earth goddess and Apu the god of the mountains for protection.

small stone and carry it for a short distance to the top of the ridge. They would then add the stone to an existing apacheta. With this papa Alberto took a small stone out of his pocket and carefully added it to the smallest apacheta nearby. 'Just for luck.' He said with a smile.

Carlos looked around at the wide view he had of the mountains and the valley. Back where they had come from and north of their trail was a broad, flat plain containing a salina[21] with a small lake. In the water was a small flock of flamingos.

Do you know what flamingos are?" Garcia asked the children.

---

[21] Salt lake or flats formed by the hot, volcanic springs along the altiplano

"They are large pink and white birds with long skinny legs. They like to walk in the waters of the salinas with their beaks upside down to catch the small creatures which live in the saltwater. Some say that their pink colour is caused by these little pink creatures which they eat."

"Then Maria will turn yellow because she eats many bananas" interjected Rodrigo with a grin. The children laughed at this idea, even little Maria who was a good-natured soul.

"Perhaps" continued Garcia. "Her face looks nice and pink to me and flamingos are very beautiful. All of the children laughed and Maria flushed an even deeper shade of pink.

Garcia continued his story. "Higher up the trail, on another ridge, Carlos saw a small herd of vicuña. They were smaller than the llamas and their wool was shorter and a light brown in colour except for white tuffs below their necks and body. 'Look Papa, vicuñas!' Carlos exclaimed. Papa nodded and smiled and said that they had come from the salina in the valley where they licked salt and were now going up into the mountains to their high pastures. Sumaq thought that they were very handsome and they were free to roam the mountains. She was very envious. Sinchi put his nose in the air and gave a superior snort." The children all laughed.

"So after lunch had been taken, Papa Alberto collected all of the llamas and tied their ropes one after each other and then to Sinchi's harness and then they again set off up the trail towards the high mountains.

It was very late in the afternoon and Inti had hidden behind the snow-capped peaks in front of their trail. By now they were in another wide valley with very steep sides of bare rock, small slopes where the rocks had slipped down and sometimes grass where mountain springs trickled from the walls. Up the valley the peaks seemed to be higher and covered in more snow. Carlos could also see a little river of ice coming from a flat field of snow which had formed on the side of the tallest mountain. There were many smaller valleys going this way and that and a little river gurgled its way over a bed of large rocks down the valley from where they had come.

Eventually they stopped where a wide circle had been cleared in the stones and boulders of the valley floor near the trail. This circle had been used many times by travellers along the trail, it was a good place to sleep. There was a small circular pen made from rocks into which Papa Alberto herded the llamas. Little Sumaq was afraid to go into the small pen with the big llama so she was allowed to stay outside. Now Papa Alberto gave Carlos some very firm instructions.

'You must care for your alpaca. Tie her securely to one of the Keñua[22] bushes so that she does not run away, but give her some extra rope so that she can lie down.'

---

[22] Small shrubs with a twisted brown trunk and stubby branches with clumps of dark green leaves. They can be found over 5000 m as smaller bushes but are usually bigger at lower altitudes.

Carlos tethered his little alpaca under a bush and gave her a hug and wished her a good night sleep. He then walked along the trail looking for dried dung for the fire which Abuelo Tomás had started with sticks in a small stone fireplace at the edge of their sleeping circle. Soon he had cooked a fine stew made from dried potatoes and corn, beans and chillies and a little charqui which is died meat. All of this he had carried on his back in his q'ipirina.

It was cold and the darkness of the night had closed in around them. The warm glow of the fire gave them some warmth and comfort. Papa Alberto had cut some of the tuffs of ichu[23] grass and spread it on one side of the circle for their bed.

[23] A thin grass, often called 'feather grass' which grows in large clumps high in the Andes and is a source of food for the vicuñas and guanacos.

Onto this he spread one of the woven blankets that Mama Isadora had made. They would be warm tonight, huddled together under their blankets.

After cleaning their plates and packing their supplies back into the packs, Papa Alberto said prayers to God and the Virgin for the family back home and for their safe journey the next day. Then they pulled up their blankets and went to sleep. Carlos lay down and looked up at the clear dark sky with its sparkling cover of stars and the cold night wind blowing gently on his face. He looked up and saw the great river of stars called by the Ancients Mayu, which we call the Milky Way. Abuelo Tomás was already softly snoring, so Carlos rolled over and went to sleep.

Now there was something that woke little Carlos some time later, His father and grandfather were still fast asleep. The sky was still clear but now Mama Killa's[24] face shone fully on the country so Carlos could see the whole valley and the moonlight sparkled on the snowy white peaks of the mountains. Something was wrong but he did not know what it was. He quietly moved his blankets and crept away from his father's side. He put on his sandals, poncho and warm chullo and climbed up onto a rock at the edge of their sleeping circle. He looked at the rock pen where the llamas were sleeping but all was quiet. He looked over to the bush where Sumaq was sleeping. She was not there! Where had she gone, children?"

[24] Quechua *mama* mother, *killa* moon, "Mother Moon"

The children looked at each other and Rodrigo shrugged his shoulders and pouted. Little Sofia said "She might have gone home to her mama?"

"But no, she did not go back down the valley to her mama. Where could she have gone?" asked Garcia.

"She has run off to join the wild vicuñas" snorted Sinchi, his head now resting on the top stones of the pen, but all Carlos heard was his snorting and a series of trilled hoots.

"Carlos was very afraid for little Sumaq. She had broken her rope and had run away. Alpacas sometimes do that if they are not kept in their pen." continued Garcia.

Now Carlos was a very smart boy. He also thought that Sumaq may have gone to look for the wild vicuñas which they had earlier seen going up into the mountains to their high pastures. He thought that Sumaq was a naughty alpaca and blamed himself for not tying the rope strongly. But what should he do? Should he wake Papa Alberto and Abuelo Tomás and get them to look for Sumaq? No. Carlos had been told by his father that Sumaq was his responsibility and must be cared for at all times. So Carlos did a foolish thing. He decided to go and look for his little lost alpaca. After all, the Moon was full and bright and he could see for a long way. Perhaps she is just over that ridge he thought. So he quietly crept away from the sleeping circle and carefully treaded his way between the stones and the tuffs of grass and began to climb the slope up to the ridge. It was a long climb because there was no trail. There were many large rocks which had rolled down from the tall peaks above and many thorny bushes and small cacti. Eventually Carlos reached the top and looked around. The brightness of Mama Killa allowed him to see a long way up the valley but there was no sign of Sumaq. Perhaps she went down the valley, he thought. No. She would climb higher to look for the vicuñas, so Carlos slowly headed along the ridge higher into the steep valley.

When he thought that he would not be heard by his father and grandfather, he called out 'Sumaq! Sumaq! But there was nothing except the gentle sound of the wind blowing down the valley.

Carlos was so concerned for his little alpaca that he did not think that this was a dangerous place. There were snakes and spiders, and sometimes even pumas would come up into the high mountains looking for young vicuñas. So Carlos kept on walking. Up the valley, over the rocks which had fallen down and through the thorny bushes. Once he even came upon a small patch of snow and ice which had not melted because it was always in shadow, He carefully trod across the glistening white surface; each foot being placed flat upon the surface so he would not slip. He did not know how long he had been walking but now he was very uncertain as to where he was. 'Sumaq! Sumaq! He called, but still there was only the sound of Wayra wind.

Now Sumaq had indeed found the small herd of vicuñas high up on the ridge. They had settled down for the night and were all fast asleep – except for the biggest vicuña who always kept one eye open for danger. He saw little Sumaq coming up the ridge so he jumped up and gave a warning snort, wagging his tail so that his whole body shook. Sumaq stopped suddenly and gave a reassuring call which was like a low humming sound as if to say 'May I come and join your herd?' The vicuñas were all awake and standing now and they looked at little Sumaq with very dark expressions."

Garcia pulled a deep frown and looked around at the children who all laughed.

Garcia then continued his story by making sounds like those that vicuñas make when distressed – a series of high-pitched sounds. "Squeeku, squeeku, squeeku" said Garcia in a loud voice which again brought laughter from the children.

"The vicuñas quickly ran off a short distance then stopped and again looked at Sumaq. 'Go away. You are just a little alpaca and belong to the Humans. You are not a mountain vicuña.' They said and turned to run off over the ridge.

Little Sumaq was sad and unwanted. She had so much wanted to be a vicuña and roam free in the mountains. But they were right. She was only a little alpaca and could never be a wild vicuña and roam the mountains. She suddenly felt afraid and lonely.

Just then, a long way off down the valley in the clear air she heard her name. 'Sumaq! Sumaq!' It was her Boy calling her. What was he doing up on the ridge? Here was someone who did want her, so she quickly turned and ran along the ridge down the valley.

Carlos was down in the valley and a long way from where his father and grandfather were sleeping. In fact he was not sure where he was. He only knew that he was lost and cold. He was very sad. He had lost his little alpaca Sumaq and now he too was lost. The wind was now colder and coming off the snow of the high peaks up the valley.

He sat down upon a small rock and pulled his chullo down around his ears and his poncho up around his knees and felt very sorry for himself. Suddenly he heard a number of small humming sounds coming from up the valley. He looked up and saw in the moonlight a little white shape with long spindly legs picking its way through the small bushes. 'Sumaq!' he cried and jumped up and ran to his little alpaca and gave her a big hug. She was also very happy to see her Boy and nuzzled her head into his chest with a soft hum.

It was getting cold but Carlos had found his little alpaca and was no longer afraid. He gathered up several armfuls of the dried grasses around them and made a small bed in the shelter of a large rock. He led Sumaq to the shelter and gathered her legs so that she lay down on the grass. Carlos sat down against her warm fur and spread his poncho over his body and her feet. 'Time to sleep now, Sumaq." he said, and the little alpaca tucked her long neck and face into her Boy's chest and was happy.

It seemed only like a short time but they had been sleeping for many hours when the first warm rays of Inti came up over the distant mountains down the valley and woke Carlos up. Sumaq was standing nearby eating some grass. Carlos was cold in the morning air and his body was very stiff from lying on the thin bed of grass but he was happy to see Sumaq.

Sumaq saw that her Boy was awake and gave a little snort. She walked off down the ridge a little distance and turned and looked at Carlos as if to say 'come on, this the way home!' Carlos went to her and she moved off again, turned her heard and snorted. Carlos knew then that Sumaq knew where she was going so he followed her down the ridge, though the many small boulders and bushes and across the small patch of snow. After a short time, Sumaq had found the track which led down the valley and so they were able to walk with more confidence.

The light was getting brighter now and in the far distance Carlos could see a lone figure walking up the track to meet them. It was Papa Alberto. Carlos was frightened. What would his Papa do because he had disobeyed and had run off?"

Garcia looked around at the children with a grim face.

"He will get a hiding!" stated Rodrigo with some authority.

"He will give his little boy a big hug because he has found him safe and well." said Maria with more compassion.

"Yes, my child." Garcia beamed at the little girl. "That is exactly what he did...in fact he ran up the track to meet his son and threw his arms around him and gave him a big hug.

'I have found you at last.' Papa Alberto said with tears in his eyes. 'And you have found your little alpaca!' He said, giving Sumaq a pat on her head. 'You were wrong to have gone searching by yourself. Next time we all look together and little Sumaq should not be allowed to go up into the dangerous mountains by herself.'

With that, Papa Alberto patted Sumaq to go on down the track before them and he took Carlos' hand and they both walked together. 'Abuelo Tomás will be worried about us but he will have some hot mate[25] and cakes.'

[25] Tea, mate de coca which is tea made from coca leaves

And so they went back down the mountain with the morning light of Inti smiling upon them; the little lost alpaca who had found that she was happy to be what she was and not something which she could not be, and the little boy who had found his alpaca and had had his first night in the mountains alone."

El sexto carta – el lustrabota
(The sixth letter – the shoe-shine boy)

It was after dinner, a few nights ago, and Comandante Castillo and I had retired from the table after an excellent meal. Teniente Rivera, the Comandante's Second and the only other officer in the hacienda, left as was his custom.

As we settled down in the large armchairs in front of the fire, for it was becoming cold at night, the Comandante poured out a generous glass of a fine Colheita[1] and leaned over towards me.

"You know, Colonel, I am sometimes worried about that young man. He is a good administrator and comes from a

---

[1] Pronounced [col-ay-ta], is a tawny port from a single vintage aged for at least seven years in the barrel.

fine military family but he is not happy here."

"He seems to carry himself well and is quite respectful to me. The men seemed to respect him also." I remarked.

"Yes, that is true." The Comandante continued. "He is generally a good officer for such a young man, but I feel that he thinks that being a junior supply officer is below his station. He is of Argentine birth and his father was a well-respected Colonel in their army; a man with a good reputation as a leader in the field and one who fought bravely in several campaigns."

"Ah! I understand his problem" I commented." He is like many young men of this generation. He wants everything at once and has too much pride to want to start at the bottom and work for the exalted status which is assumed owed to him."

"Oh yes, Colonel" he replied." It seems to be the expectation of our young people to want now what their parents took years to gain through hard work."
I was in a deep, satisfied philosophical mood, which is a good state for a Philosopher to be in and so I recounted an episode of my early life to illustrate my thoughts. "I have found, Don Antonio, that it is not the work that a person does which is the value of their life, but how they perform that work. Luckily I found this truth when I was still a young man. May I be permitted to tell you my story?"

"I would be honoured, Senor, if you would." said the Comandante refilling my empty glass with another generous measure of his fine port.

I continued with my story.

"A very long time ago; too long for me to mention in years, I too was a young officer with all of the pride and thoughts of future grandeur which no doubt reside in Teniente Rivera's mind. Although I was commissioned into the Militia, my Colonel had requested that I accompany him and another senior officer to a conference in the Bolivian capital of La Paz. I suspect that my father's political connections had something to do with this. Have you been to La Paz, Don Antonio?"

"Ah yes! The beautiful city of Nuestra Señora de La Paz[2]. I have been there once, but it was too high and enclosed for my liking" commented the Comandante.

"Oh!" I replied in mock horror. "You do not like our mountains! Yes, La Paz is a beautiful city and being set at the bottom of a long, deep canyon surrounded by mountains and the altiplano, it can be daunting. Especially if there are earth tremors which are common enough there.

Well, to continue; I had been staying with my cousins in Puno, the city on the shores of Lake Titicaca well to the south of my home in Cuzco. The new railway

---

[2] In English, "Our Lady of the Peace" is the full name of this city, still the most well-known city in Bolivia and site of many of its financial institutions, although Santa Cruz de la Sierra is now the biggest city and Sucre is its capital.

line from Juliaca[3] to Cuzco is still under construction, so most of the passenger transportation is by coach, usually a four-in-hand[4]. This journey from Puno to La Paz is an adventure in itself.

I joined by colleagues very early the next morning at the staging post on the Avenida[5] Simon Bolivar; it would not be good for a young Alférez[6] to be late. We were lucky in that there were not many travellers that morning so the three of us could ride inside the coach.

Off we started. Out of the city and south along the edge of the lake our coach rattled. Past small fields planted between

[3] [hooly-ARCHA] a town on the lake about 40 km north of Puno
[4] A coach pulled by four horses or mules and controlled by one driver. They could seat 4 to 8 passengers and usually carried another coachman at the rear or with the driver.
[5] Avenue
[6] Ensign – the lowest rank of officer

the road and the water with an early morning mist drifting across the still lake. We travelled inland away from the water and through the small village of Ilave, the main centre of the Aymara people. Soon the lake reappeared as we came over a small hill and down into the circular valley that held the fishing town of Juli[7]. This is a very picturesque town, with many adobe buildings and sometimes called the 'Rome of the Altiplano' because of its many churches. The town is nestled within high surrounding hills around the central plaza which is flanked by the large church of Saint John the Lateran. This is a large building constructed in adobe with a roof of red tiles. Inside, there is a large gilt and silver altar piece and the side walls are covered with many large and

[7] Pronounced [hooli]

beautiful paintings in the style of the Italian and Cuzco Schools, framed in gold and silver.

We stopped here for a passable lunch of soup, rolls and fish before continuing on our journey around the edge of the lake until we came to the village of Yunguyo in the late afternoon. Here we were obliged climb out of the coach and walk the last hundred metres or so up a long sloping hill to the Bolivian border. Our coach continued up the hill past us, no doubt to be searched by the border guards.

We passed under a large, crudely-constructed arch which held a sign 'Bienvenidos a Bolivia'[8] and into the Bolivian town of Kasuni. Here we were

---

[8] 'Welcome to Bolivia'

ushered into the military post where our papers were closely examined by the Border Guards. As our papers were in order and we held a passport from the Bolivian military, we had a friendly welcome. This was not the case for our fellow travellers, who were both foreigners and who were subjected to many questions and requests for additional papers.

Eventually we were all allowed to continue on our way for another hour when we came into the town of Copacabana where we were to stay the night. This town is a very significant religious site of early Aymara people and of the Incas who adopted the Aymara veneration. Its name is thought to have come from the Aymara 'kota kawana' meaning 'a view of the lake'[9] and on one side of the small but pleasant Plaza de Armes, are the impressive white buildings of the Basilica of Our Lady of Copacabana. It is interesting to note that our neighbours in Brazil have given a beach in their city of Rio de Janeiro the very same name of Copacabana. One may think that a Chechua-speaking wit has passed a sarcastic comment on the peaceful nature of the mighty Atlantic Ocean there, but that is unlikely considering the Ocean's storms. No, the real reason of why an Aymara term should be given to a Brazilian beach is that more recently a chapel was built there to hold a replica of the same statue of Our Lady of Copacabana which

[9] There is also a suggestion that it may have been derived from 'Kotakawana, a god of fertility in ancient Andean mythology,

resides in the Basilica of the Bolivian town.

Copacabana in Bolivia is a charming lakeside town. Like many towns on the Lake it is nestled in a curve of hills whose slopes come steeply down to meet the water. Apart from its attraction as a religious site both to Christianity and also to the older religion, it is noted for its fishing and relaxed atmosphere. The town also provides access to nearby islands in the Lake. These are the Isla del Sol and the Isla de la Luna; the islands of the Sun and the Moon. The Isla del Sol is venerated as the birthplace of Inti the Incan god of the sun, as well as the place from which the first Inca, Manco Cápac[10]came. The Isla de la Luna is also

10 From the Quechua: Manqu Qhapaq - 'the royal founder' who also founded Cuzco.

regarded as the place where Viracocha[11]commanded the first rising of the moon, Mama Killa.

It being late afternoon, the coach stopped at a small posada[12] and staging post for the night. This gave me some small opportunity to explore the town. As the posada was near the centre of the town, being only a few streets from the Plaza de Armes, I decided to walk down the narrow cobbled street to the lake. There were numerous small shops and cafes along the street and the people's smiles were friendly. At the end of the street was the harbour front – or so it was called. This consisted of a wide, curved bay which had many small jetties –

[11] The pre-Incan creator god who also emerged from Lake Titicaca and created the Sun and the Moon
[12] Posada – a small inn, usually owned by a family

narrow timber planks – running out into the water. At some there were several small boats tied up. These were all crude affairs made of roughly hewn planks that were painted in a variety of bright colours. Out on the still, dark blue waters of the lake, was a traditional reed boat from which its two occupants were fishing. This was a small craft, but I am told that they could be constructed up to thirty metres in length with a large superstructure of two stories on their central platform. These larger craft often had their bows decorated with the heads of the puma. The puma is one of the three sacred animals of the Andinos; the other two being the serpent and the condor. They are made from the totora reeds which grow in abundance all around the lake. These are bound tightly together into long bundles and then stitched together to form the hulls of the craft. Canes or sticks are often lashed on top to make a high deck which keeps the occupants very dry. The small fishing boat which I observed this morning was one of the smaller kind with a simpler construction of bound reeds meeting at a simple, raised bow. The fishermen were using long poles to propel their craft towards the shore after a long afternoon's fishing.

On the far side and under the shadow of Cerro Calvario[13] is a small building surrounded by a stone wall containing a small square and a flagstaff with the Bolivian flag. This is the local unit of the Bolivian Navy which is meant to protect this side of the border and prevent smuggling across the lake to Peru. I am

[13] Calvary Hill – a prominent landmark of Copacabana, now a religious shrine with a pathway following the Stations of the Cross

told that there is also a lucrative smuggling trade across the nearby border across the Lake to Puno, but that is to be expected when the colonizing authorities arbitrarily mark borders across traditional trade routes of the indigenous people. It is apparently a difficult task to prevent this smuggling considering the fact that many people on both sides of the border share a common heritage and in many cases are related. Still, the governments try to prevent it, but life goes on.

That night, my colleagues and I dined at our posada on beautifully-cooked fish, potatoes, corn and beans with an excellent bottle of the local cerveza[14]. From our vantage point, for the dining

[14] Beer - made in the European style as opposed to chicha which is traditional corn beer.

area of the posada was on an upper roof balcony, we could see a distant storm moving across the lake. Heavy dark clouds moved across the lake from the east whilst the setting sun gave the sky to the west below the clouds an unearthly red glow. Large bolts of lightning struck the darkened waters which were now being agitated into a confused swell of small waves. The small boats at their moorings at the waterfront were being tossed against their piers. The stillness of the air and the electric nature of the atmosphere at our open air dining room gave the entire scene a distinctly eerie sensation and reminded me of my mother's tales of the spirits of the old religion. There was Illapa, the 'Flashing One', who as Lord of storms and lightning, controlled the forces of wind, rain, hail and snow. The Aymara of the Bolivian altiplano had a similar deity named Tunupa who was associated with the mountains, Illampu which rise abruptly to our east and Illimani further to the south of the Lake. The Inca called their mountain deities Apu and their goddess of the earth was venerated as Pachamama who also was responsible for earthquakes.

The next morning our coach set off early, climbing slowly up into the hills which surround Copacabana. The road was good, but wound tightly from one hilltop to the next, mostly with glorious views of the lake behind us. These hills were mainly devoid of trees but the pasture was green with a few small streams running down towards the lake. Across the hills cut several sharp spines of rock which had been upturned by some great upheaval in the distant past.

A few hours later, we descended into the little town of San Pedro de Tiquina, situated on a narrow strip of land opposite a broad strait of water. It was here that Lake Titicaca narrowed down to about five hundred metres. On a good map, this strait formed the neck of the puma which the ancients likened to the shape of the Lake. Further to the south, the lake opened up again to form the head of the puma. Here we were requested to alight and make our way to the waterfront where a boatman ushered us into his small craft and for a few coins took us across the water to San Pablo de Tiquina on the opposite shore. Meanwhile, our coach complete with its four horses still in harness and all of our luggage, were carefully taken on board a low punt made of large logs lashed together. Only the two boatmen were permitted on board this craft which was then slowly poled over to the San Pablo side.

After some refreshment at a small cantina facing the main plaza of the town, we again joined our coach for the last leg of our journey to La Paz. This was uneventful and was along a small section of the altiplano above the hills south of the lake with the line of snow-capped mountains to our east. It was near nightfall when our coach came to the staging post at El Alto[15]. There were a few small buildings, badly constructed, which housed the people who looked after the coach and horses and provided some poor accommodation for travellers such as us. Below us in a long valley stretching a long way further south were

[15] Meaning "The Halt" in Spanish and was the stopping place of the conquistador Alonso de Mendoza (1471-1549) the founder of the city of Nuestra Señora de La Paz in 1548. Since then, El Alto has grown to be the second biggest city of Bolivia.

the myriad lights of the city of Nuestra
Señora de La Paz over a thousand metres
below us. As the road down the narrow
ravine into the city was both steep and
narrow, we were obliged to stay the
night at el Alto.

It was still dark; just before dawn and the
rays of the sun were just backlighting the
snows on the peaks to the east. This
morning, the ostler[16] had replaced our
horses with four strong mules which
would be better in handling the coach
down the steep declines. We set off full
of trepidation, but the mules were sturdy
and the two coachmen skilled in
handling the brake. Soon we were at the
end of the ravine and happily jangling
down the narrow cobbled streets of La

16 The ostler is the person who looks after horses and hitches up the team
to a coach.

Paz. On the Avenida Illampu we stopped at a fashionable hotel built in the European style where we were to spend the night. The porter having taken our bags to our rooms and the manager having given us our keys, my enthusiasm for this new city was too much, so I bade farewell to my colleagues and went for a short walk down the avenue. The first street which I encountered was called Calle[17] Santa Cruz which ran steeply downhill to the left. It seemed to have some promise as it contained several small shops selling a variety of foods. Further down the street, the shops seemed to take on a religious tone with names such as 'Chifleria[18] of the Angels' and 'Market of the Spirits'. On closer inspection, I found that the many items

[17] Street
[18] A booth of small shop

which were on display were all of those items which were needed for the old religion. There was a great variety of painted clay statues of the many Andean deities, bags of sweet-smelling herbs and dried llama foetuses hanging from their awnings. Suddenly I recalled what I had read about La Paz. This was the famous El Mercado de las Brujas or the 'Witches Market' where practitioners of the old religion could buy what was necessary to obtain the help of the ancient deities. Here one could buy medicinal herbs for one's ailments, or have their fortune read in leaves of the coca plant, or buy the llama foetus which would be burnt at the beginning of a prayer to Pachamama, the earth goddess, so that one could receive health and prosperity for some future undertaking.

I was not horrified at these items. To be sure, some of the dried llamas, toads and other unrecognisable animal bodies were unpleasant to an educated eye with a Christian upbringing, but this is part of the wide Andean culture and has been practiced well before the Holy Fathers brought Christianity to the mountains. From my own family experience, I have witnessed my uncles performing such rituals for various requests and then go to mass and pray to Our Lady for the same thing. There seems to be a blurring of thought when it comes to Our Lady and Pachamama. Who am I to judge? It is, after all a matter of faith. But one thing is certain in the mountains; this faith is strong and guides the people in their daily tasks and they seem to be better than those whom I have met in the lowland cities whose faith seems to be somewhat narrower and less sincere.

But now, Comandante, you may be wondering about this journey and el lustrabota? Well, the journey from Puno to La Paz was very exciting for a young Militia officer and worth telling as it now leads up to my philosophical view about the ethics of honest work."

The Comandante lent across the table to light my cigar. "No, please go on. Your travels interest me a great deal. I myself have never been to that region and being lowland bred have only the local stories here in Baños to help me think how the true Andino lives."

"Thank you Don Antonio. Then I will conclude my story.

Continuing my walk down the street of the brujas with its many shops with herbs, statues and masks, I noticed a thin young man who wore a bandana around his face. He was sitting on a small wooden box and was offering to clean the shoes of all who passed. I had remembered seeing similar men as we passed the many small plazas as we came into the city. These were the local shoe-shine boys who, for a few small coins would give your boots a quick shine and then scurry off to seek a new location. They did this because they were ashamed of their work. The masks and bandanas they wore were to protect their identity. What shame would it be for a hard-working family who had moved off their poor farms into the city to have their young men work as servants cleaning the boots of strangers? Also these men were proud. Why would a young señorita[19] be attracted to a lowly shoe-shine boy?

I quickly passed him by. It was not because my boots did not need a shine. Far from it! The long journey had dulled their appearance and as an officer of the lowest rank I had no-one to polish my boots for me and perhaps I too, was ashamed of my appearance. Or perhaps I did not want to join in the young man's self-pity and use his time to perform this lowly function. I cannot recall, but I passed on down the cobbled street to where it opened out into a very large plaza. This was the Park Major also known as the Square of Saint Francis. On the corner and around to my right were several small tables with street vendors selling small trinkets and sweets. In front

19 Young lady "Miss"

at some distance was the bustling Avenida Mariscal Santa Cruz[20].

I turned the corner and walked into the plaza. At its far end and downhill was the Basilica of San Francisco, an imposing building made out of yellow stone with a large single bell tower. I went in and lit a candle in thanks for our safe journey – or perhaps as a confirmation of my faith after having passed through the Witches Market. A passing official of the church stopped and offered me his greeting. We fell into conversation for he was proud of his church. He told me that the Franciscans had been in this area before the city was founded by the conquistador Alonso de Mendoza in 1548. Their leader, Fray Francisco de Morales had been welcomed and given land by the chief of

[20] Marshal Santa Cruz Avenue

the local Aymara people. This is where a small church was built here on the banks of the Choqueyapu River. No doubt the local people were impressed by the poverty and humility of the Franciscan friars. When Don Alonzo arrived, a more substantial church was built but its roof collapsed after a heavy snowfall in 1612. In such a remote locality with more pressing matters to attend to, the church stood unfinished for over a century. Eventually construction recommenced allowing this fine building to be completed in 1758. It was named in honour of its founder, Fray Francisco de los Angeles Morales, whose remains are entombed in the church. The Sacristan, for that was the title of my new friend, took me for a walk around the magnificent interior then up a very narrow flight of stairs to the first storey of the imposing bell tower which was completed in 1885. Here was a wide vista of the city which sloped away down the long valley to the south and into the centre of commerce with its European buildings made of fine stone. In the distance were the snow-capped peaks of La Paz's dominant mountain, Illimani. This name comes from an Aymara word meaning 'water bearer', it is considered the queen of the mountain deities within Bolivia.

After my tour of the Basilica, I exited the beautifully ornate doors out into the plaza which bears the same name. I had walked only a few paces when I was struck by the sight of a rather ornate chair nestling under the trees to one side of the plaza. Here was another shoe-shine stand but one with a great difference. Here was no simple wooden box upon which el lustrabota kept his few meagre tools and then used it as a footrest for his customers. Here was a proud, upright chair of substantial proportions and comfort. It even had a small canopy which jutted out over the head of the customer to afford some protection from the sun. The shoe-shine boy was also different. To use the term 'boy' would be an insult. This man was of about middle age and unlike his younger competitors wore no mask to hide his face which had been darkened and lined with many years out in the elements.

Now, my boots were black riding boots, typical of the officer class, they had had much neglect over the last few days. Even in the barracks, a young militia officer must clean his own boots and rarely has the services of a servant to perform this duty for him. I waited until the shoe-shiner had finished with his last customer, then I walked over and sat down with a cheerful 'Buenos dias, Señor'. He returned my morning salutation with a smile and he beckoned me to be seated. I then noticed that my boots rested upon a small dias upon which was proudly printed the man's name, Ignacio.

'It is a fine day, Ignacio'. I said.

'Si, Señor. Fine enough for some nice shiny boots.' He laughed.

With that he began his art; for I soon found that he applied his trade with the skill, perfection and care of an artisan. This was no mere lustrabota who quickly gave one's shoes a cursory shine and then took your money. This man loved his work and took professional pride in every action.

First he brushed over my boots with a fine horse-hair brush to remove the surface dust. It had a finely carved handle of some Andean design. Next he gently rubbed over the boots with a soft, damp cloth to continue the removal of any dust. He then exchanged this cloth for another and, dipping it into a tin of a creamy mixture he then continued the cleaning process. He wiped this off using a slow circular motion using another, moistened cloth. After the boots had been thoroughly cleaned, he then applied another soft paste which was probably a leather restorer. This he also rubbed in with a slow, circular motion.

These were not his only actions. During this initial cleaning procedure he had a number of visitors who would drop a few coins into an ornate wooden box by his side from which Ignacio would extract a broad ticket. This must be a lottery of a kind common to these parts. These acts were usually accompanied by the usual morning salutations; 'Buenos dias, Ignacio' most would say because it was obvious that this lustrabota was a well-known and popular figure in the Plaza de San Francisco.

For my part it was also relaxing to sit in this big, comfortable chair whilst my boots were receiving such careful treatment. I had the time to sit back and watch the passing activities in the plaza and on the busy avenue beyond. Here were the usual passing parade of people going about their business: the office workers in their faded dark suits; the ladies in their bright village dresses selling a variety of foods and trinkets from their stalls which lined one side of the plaza; and the carriages, hand-carts and mounted citizens moving up and down the broad Avenida Mariscal Santa Cruz.

Ignacio continued his ministrations with the application of a lustrous black polish which he kept in another can which he had carefully opened. He used a small, circular brush which also had the same motifs carved on its handle. He rubbed in the polish with a soft circular motion, making sure that it penetrated all of the creases of the leather and grooves around the edge of the sole. Then he gave the entire surface of both boots a vigorous lathing with a soft leather cloth. This was the most extensive part of the treatment and was followed up with more polishing with a hand glove which looked like alpaca wool. Finally he polished the rims of the sole of the boot with protective oil.

I was amazed at both his care and rapid dexterity. This man had practiced his art over many years and was proud of his work. It was also clear that the local community also shared in his pride and passion for I had noticed that several other men waited under the trees ready to enjoy the craftsman's skills.

Well! There you have it, Comandante. The story of the lustrabota of La Paz. Perhaps you may be able to gently remind the young Teniente that it is not the type of work that matters but how it is done that shows the worth of a person. Also, as my acquaintance with the good Ignacio taught me, the true professional is also usually happy in themselves for doing such a professional job."

The old Comandante smiled and leaned back in his chair and took a long draw on his cigar. "Perhaps you are right Colonel. Perhaps you are right."

El séptima carta - a fin del mondo

(The seventh letter – at the end of the World)

You may recall that I mentioned Teniente Gabriel Rivera Peña in a previous letter. He is the young Supply Officer for the hacienda and the second-in-command to the Comandante. You will recall also that Don Antonio was concerned about this man's welfare as he was unhappy at doing such a lowly task as looking after the supplies here.

It was the custom of Teniente Rivera to leave the dinner table immediately after his evening meal and not spend much time with myself and his senior officer in social interaction. Never-the-less, from what the Comandante has said and of his general dealings about the hacienda, it is obvious that the young man has a great respect and devotion to his older superior officer.

One night after dinner and after the Teniente had left on the usual excuse that he had the next day's administration to attend, Don Antonio and I retired to our lounge chairs as usual for a quiet cigar and some wine.

I remarked that the Teniente seemed to avoid the socialisation which was often common in an Officers' Mess and enquired if he had difficulties in mixing with other officers. The Comandante replied that, from his observations the Teniente interacted well with the soldiers and staff of the hacienda and was very competent at his job, but that he lacked the personality traits which made some officers popular and good leaders. To be sure, Teniente Rivera was generally liked by the people here but more as a pleasant and inoffensive young man rather than a superior officer and leader of men.

"Perhaps it has to do with his background?" the Comandante suggested. "You know that he was born in Argentina and comes from a well-respected military family."

"You may be right" I replied. "Perhaps he feels that he does not belong in the uniform of Ecuador".

"Possibly" the Comandante replied whilst refilling his glass. "His family has been in our country for several years and are now recognised as respected citizens in this country. I believe that his father was once a well-connected Colonel in the army of the Argentine; an engineer by all accounts, but some political change caused them to immigrate north. We do not discuss this, the Teniente and I, but who knows? As my guest and a soldier from another country, you may want to learn more of his life. That is, if you are the philosopher I think you are?" he said with his usual wise smile.

It was a few days later, when I was taking my usual morning walk around the colonnades of the two courtyards of the hacienda when I saw the young man in question sitting on one of the small, ornate benches in the outer courtyard. He was reading a letter but had obviously finished and had put it down as I approached.

"Buenos dias, Teniente[1]." I said. The young officer jumped to his feet and gave a quick salute. This was probably more of a military reaction as he had become used to my existence as a guest (shall we say) at San Rafael.

"Oh, please be seated." I said with a smile. "It is too fine a morning to be formal. May I sit with you?"

He sat down slowly and gave a shy smile. "Yes, please do" he said, waving his hand over the vacant seat. "My duties for the morning are over until the supply wagon comes."

I sat and offered the Teniente one of Don Antonio's fine cigars. I nodded at the

---

[1] Good morning, Lieutenant

letter which he had placed on the bench. "Good news, I trust?"

"Oh Si, Colonel" he grinned. "My sister, Louisa is getting married!"

"Ah. That is wonderful." I replied. The Comandante mentioned in passing that you had been born in Argentina. Is the wedding to be performed there?"

"No, Señor. It will be at our home in Bahia de Caraquez which is on the coast northwest of Quito" he replied. "It is true that I was born in Argentina. Both my sisters and I were born in Buenos Aires[2] but our family moved to Ecuador many years ago."

[2] Buenos Aires is located on the western shore of the estuary of the Río de la Plata, and its name can be translated as "good airs" or "fair winds" , but the original meaning intended by the founders in the 16th century, was the later by the use of the original name "Nuestra Señora Santa María del Buen Ayre" or "Our Lady Saint Mary of the Good Winds"

"Buenos Aires - that is a beautiful city." I said with an expansive puff of my cigar. "Some call it the 'Paris of the South' but – you know- I have been in both cities and I think that such a label is unfair to those who live in that fine capital of your homeland. Paris is vibrant. That is for certain, but Buenos Aires has more life in it. The people live for life. The music is intoxicating and there seems to be that Latino spirit which the French do not possess. They get too melancholy at times but we in South America do not. We get sad. We get excited but we live life. If we do not like something, we protest, sometimes we have a revolution, but we never sit about in a pool of sadness."

Teniente Rivera laughed at my homespun philosophy.

"That is true, mi Colonel! It is the same all over this great continent.

You are from a military family?" I enquired, knowing full well that this was the case but hoping to draw the young man into conversation.

"I am, Colonel. My father was also a Colonel in the Engineers and we lived in a fine house in Buenos Aires – in the barrio[3] Recoleta – not far from its famous cemetery. Do you know it, Señor?"

"No" I replied. "Unfortunately my stay in your fair city was but a brief one. I stayed in a small apartment on Avenida Rivadavio in the barrio Caballito and then only as a young tourista. I was impressed by the European buildings

[3] Suburb or local area

and broad avenues. The food and the late night music were very enticing, especially for a young man from the mountains. Although I did notice that some of the wall slogans painted here and there championed the cause of los indios[4].

"Unfortunately that sometimes is the case, Colonel" the young man replied. "We porteños[5] sometimes forget the rights of our local peoples. Our city and much of the country has been populated by European immigrants – my own family came from Galicia[6] in the late 17th

[4] The Indians – referring to the indigenous people of South America but not used necessarily in a derogatory manner.
[5] "People of the Port" is what many people in central Buenos Aires call themselves.
[6] Part of north western Spain.

Century- and so we often forget those who were here before the Conquest. Is it not the same in your country?"

"Yes" I sadly replied. "In the big cities on the coast where the Spanish settled perhaps, but in the mountains where I come from, the true Andino has a large mix of indigenous blood and the cultures of the old peoples are still very much alive. My mother's family go well back before the Spaniards arrived. But tell me Teniente, how did you become a soldier in the army of Ecuador?"

"Oh it is of little consequence" he replied shyly. "It would not interest such a man as you, Colonel – and besides, I would not like to waste your valuable time on such a lovely day."

"Where can I go? What have I to do? "I laughed. "You have forgotten that I am a prisoner in this old hacienda. My boundaries are limited and my time is empty and deficient of meaning. So tell me your story, young man. I am sure that you would have something of interest for an old man who is going nowhere."

"Well then, I will tell you a story of la tierra al final del mundo[7]." He replied with some animation and an openness which I had not seen before. "Have you been to Tierra del Fuego – the land of fire – at the very tip of our continent?"

"No" I replied. "I have never been any further south than your lovely city of Buenos Aires. To me that country is a

[7] "The land at the end of the world"

strange and magical place. Is it called the land of fire because of its volcanoes? We have those in abundance in my country."

"Oh no, Señor." He said with eyes wide with astonishment. "It was because of the many fires which the indigenous peoples, the Yamana people, lit to keep warm and to hunt for animals. The great explorer Ferdinand Magellan gave that name to the island when he passed in 1520.

My father was sent to that place to supervise the construction of docks at the new port of Ushuaia which is the biggest settlement there and also to look at the plan to build a new road from the mainland. Because it was to be a long commission, he decided to take the entire family with him. Now that, Señor, is a story worth telling."

"Please, go on. I am very interested in this story" I eagerly replied. "It seems like a new exploration of a strange land."

"Indeed, Don Hernán" the Teniente replied and I was encouraged by the use of my Christian name.

He continued. "Of course Mama and the girls were apprehensive about leaving our fine house and the civilization of our big city, but I was very excited. I was only twelve years old and eager to explore and learn everything about the world.

Father arranged for our passage on a coastal brigantine[8] as the regular clipper ships and steamers did not go to Ushuaia unless they had business there. The larger sailing ships usually went around Cape Horn further to the south past Horn Island and the steamers pass through the easier passage of the Straits of Magellan further north where the winds are unpredictable. As we were only going to Ushuaia, we had to sail down the coast of the mainland, past Tierra del Fuego to round Cabo San Diago[9].

[8] A two-masted sailing vessel with a fully square rigged sail on the foremast (front mast) and at least two sails on the main and taller mast behind, usually a square topsail and a fore-and-aft mainsail (behind the mast).
[9] Cape Saint Diago. Diago is a derivative of Santiago or Saint James. Probably named after Didacus of Alcalá, also known as Diego de San Nicolás, a Spanish Franciscan lay

To me this was a great adventure. Mother and the girls spent most of their time in their cabin – which was really the Captain's cabin which he gave to them – but Father and I spent much of our time on deck. Father would often spend his time walking the deck or talking to Capitán Delgado while I was allowed to roam the ship – usually under Father's eye, of course. The most exciting time was when all the hands – for that is what the sailors were called – were called to change the sails. Capitán Delgado would let me climb the ratlines – the rope ladders which were joined between the shrouds or standing rigging[10] which held the masts in place – before he would call

brother who served among the first group of missionaries to the Canary Islands in 1445.

[10] Permanent rope of steel cables holding the masts

the hands. This allowed me to climb up and find a secure place on the top out of the way. I was very scared at first. You can imagine a twelve year boy climbing up a fragile rope ladder fifteen metres above the deck. At the top of these ratlines were what is known as the futtock shrouds. These are cables which angle back outwards and help to keep the top in place. To climb them, one has to learn backwards out over the wáter and climb like a sloth – upside down. In some of the bigger ships there is a small hole in the side of the top called a 'lubber's hole' through which one can squeeze, but not on these smaller brigantines. I was later shown how to climb forward and around these difficult futtock shrouds and reach the top with less fear.

The Captain or First Mate would call out the order and the men would climb up the ratlines like monkeys. It was glorious to see how fast they could climb. On the foremast where the big square sails where held on the long horizontal beam called a 'yard', the sailors would run along the top of the beam and then drop down so that their feet rested on the footropes below. These were only ropes about the thickness of your finger and so they would wobble unless one locked the knees. The hands would hang over the yard and untie the gaskets or small lengths of rope which tied the big canvas sail to the yard. Once untied, they would let the sail drop freely but they had to be careful. The hands on the yards let go of the sail from the centre of the yard nearest the mast first and out near the tips of the yards last. This would allow the sail to billow out from the centre to the tip of the yard. To do the reverse often meant that unlucky sailors at the ends of the yards may be pushed off the footropes by the billowing sail.

Below on the deck, another group of hands – usually a watch or half-watch as they are called, would line up along the sheets[11] which are the ropes attached to the bottom corners of the sail on either side of the deck and haul the sails down to be secured to the sides of the deck by wrapping the sheet around a belaying pin.

The other sails on the brigantine such as the gibs which run from the bowsprit at

[11] Sheets are ropes which are used to haul and control sails. With the Halyards (haul yards), they form part of the running rigging of a ship.

the bow or front of the ship to high on the foremast are also controlled by the deck watches. Watching a change of sail was very exciting but hard work for the crew, especially if they were called out late in the night or during a rainsquall or storm. When the sea was rough, Father would not let me go out on deck.

It took us over a week to round Cabo San Diago and turn west into the quiet waters of the Beagle Channel which eventually passes into the Pacific Ocean. You have heard of this Channel, Don Hernán?"

"Yes" I replied. "If my Natural Philosophy serves me correct it was named after the British research ship the *Beagle* which carried the great Naturalist

Charles Darwin on his voyage around the world."

"That is right." Replied the Teniente, "that was in 1833 when he visited that part of the world. But it was not until 1871 when an English mission was established at what is now the town of Ushuaia. The Argentine government wanted to establish a port and penal settlement there a few years later and this is why my father was sent. We arrived in 1876 when it was very primitive. There were a few small huts and the English Mission buildings and the roads were all dirt and often muddy, but oh! The country was beautiful. The large bay – did I tell you that the name 'Ushuaia' comes from the local Yámana's words *ush* and *waia* meaning 'deep bay' - stretches out to the channel and the hills of what is now Chile to the south but is ringed all around behind the settlement by steep, tall peaks which usually are snow-capped. It is a beautiful place in summer and spring but it has much too much snow in winter while the winds from Antarctica in the autumn are bleak.

Our family found a small but comfortable house on the Avenida San Martin, not far from the waterfront. Of course Mamma missed having all of her servants but she was happy with just her maid and we were able to obtain a cook from the local people. I went to school at the English Mission. There were a number of us older children who had an Argentine teacher, Señora Alonso who, like Father was very passionate about the mistreatment of the indigenous people, the Yámana people.

I had a friend called Alejandro at the Mission. He was of the Yámana and about my age. His father was a local leader who believed that his people would only survive if they had a European education. The two of us had many great adventures together. His father had settled into a small house up near the tree line behind the town but he and his people, including Alejandro would often move further inland to hunt. This was their custom, you see.

On fine summer's days, Alejandro and I would walk up the track that winds up from the town and past the tree line into the rocks and snow. Up there was a glacier, a small river of ice and a small flat valley of snow. Of course we would not tell our fathers about our little trips — it was a secret between us. I would tell

Father that I was going up the hill to visit Alejandro, and he would tell his father that he was going down into the town to visit me. What fun we had!

At the Mission, Dona Maria our teacher would tell us all sorts of wondrous stories about the mountains and the people of the Pampas[12]. Especially stories about the wild gauchos. Do you know about the gauchos, Don Hernán?"

"No." I replied. "I have heard of them, of course but know very little about them." I had been very interested in hearing of the life of this young man. This had been the first time that he had shown his personal side. Whether he was uncomfortable at making conversation

[12] From the Quechua *'pampa'*, meaning "plain" are the fertile South American grassy lowlands which cover much of southern Argentina.

with a strange senior officer, especially one who is a prisoner of his country, or if he was simply a shy young man, I do not know, but the letter from his family was certainly a reason to be more carefree. "They are like the North American cowboys, I believe?"

"Oh, no, Señor". He replied. "They are much more colourful and romantic than the cowboys of the North Americans. They are mere vaqueros,[13] but a gaucho is a skilled horseman, brave, unruly and always a colourful character. They are a national symbol and are greatly admired and renowned for their deeds. They are not mere herders of cattle, even if that is their main occupation."

---

[13] The term 'vaquero' is derived from the Spanish word from 'vaca', meaning 'cow and are mounted cow herders.

"Of course we have cattle in my country." I said. "But nothing like the herds in Argentina. My country has few grassy plains to support such large herds like they have on your estancias[14]. But please go on. I am very interested to hear about your gauchos"

The young man smiled with some personal pride "Thank you, Señor. Would you like to hear about one of our most famous gauchos? It is a most interesting story, especially for a philosopher like yourself."

"Ah, you flatter me, Teniente." I laughed." But yes, I would very much like to hear your story. Please go on."

---

[14] Large cattle estates or ranches.

"Well then, Don Hernán." He said. "Listen to this story for it has romance, adventure and faith, all mixed together! This story was told to us at the Mission by Dona Maria, our teacher who had arrived in Ushuaia only a few years before my family arrived. Have you heard of the English legend of Robin Hood?"

"Indeed I have" I replied.

"Well then this is about the 'Robin Hood' of Argentina but unlike the English story, this is the true story of Gauchito[15] Gil, a legendary character of Argentina who is regarded as the most prominent folk hero in that country. Father also knew of him, for the gaucho was born in

[15] "Little Gaucho"

Mercedes, a town just to the west of Buenos Aires, and so he was also able to tell me some of Gauchito Gil's history. It was a very popular story whilst he lived and became more exciting after he died, which was only two years before we came to Ushuaia. His life was happening when I was a boy in Buenos Aires, but it was not as popular there as in the countryside, because Buenos Aires was an independent city and often argued with the large landowners and caudillos[16]. Besides, I had other interests as a small boy and any such stories passed through my brain very quickly. It was not until we moved out of the city to Ushuaia that Dona Maria's stories of the

[16] A vague term often poorly defined but generally meaning a strong leader who exercised military power. There were many such caudillos in Argentina in the 19th century who were often owners of large estancias or regions and who often fought with the national government.

gauchito's romantic life found a place in my heart. She said that he was the embodiment of many of the best virtues such as charity, brotherly love, obedience to a higher moral standard, defence of outcasts and the poor and of course defiance of corrupt authority. Father, being a soldier was well-acquainted with the more sober facts of Gauchito Gil's life. Well, to the story!

It is said that he was born in Pay Ubre which is near what is now the town of Mercedes in Corrientes Province just west of Buenos Aires, somewhere about 1840 as Antonio Gil Núñez and that he was a typical gaucho. Dona Maria had read many stories in the newspapers about him and described him as being a stocky man with long black hair and broad moustacios. He wore a loose pale-blue shirt, often rolled up past his elbows with a red bandana[17] and long, cream-coloured accordion-pleated trousers, called bombachas de campo, which are buttoned at the ankles and cover the tops of high leather boots. Around his waist he wore a chiripa, a woolen poncho often fastened between his legs and held by a red sash around his waist. In cold weather, this could also be worn as a true poncho covering his upper body. He also carried the lasso, as well as a long knife in a silver scabbard kept in his sash behind his back. He also carried the boleadoras. Some people call these bolas which are made of leather cords separated to hold three iron balls or stones at their ends. This can be thrown

[17] Large neckerchief of red cotton folded into a triangle and worn around the neck or over the face in dust clouds.

at the legs of an animal to entwine and immobilize it. He must have cut a gallant figure, but then that is the style of the gaucho!

Estrella Díaz de Miraflores, so the story goes, was a widow and the wealthy owner of the estancia upon which Gil worked. It was said that the dashing gaucho fell in love but her brothers thought that it was very improper for a woman of wealth and fine breeding to sully herself with a gaucho. Indeed, it certainly riled the local police commissioner, who himself had eyes for the widow. He conspired with Doña Estrella's brothers to frame Gil for robbery and get rid of him. Hearing of this plot, Gil fled the estancia and joined the army.

Now at that time in 1864, the political climate of the region was extremely volatile. It was also the year in which I was born. There had been some dispute between Paraguay and Brazil which had also helped to change the government in Uruguay. The dictator of Paraguay, Francisco Solano López, feeling that his position was threatened, declared war on Brazil. López's action was viewed by many as aggression for self and national aggrandizement as he had the largest army in all of South America. To counter this aggression, the president of Argentina, Bartolomé Mitre made an alliance with the new government of Uruguay and joined Brazil against Paraguay. This was called the War of the Triple Alliance. This may seem a bad move by the three countries of the alliance all of which had been involved in other wars just prior to this. And don't forget that Paraguay under their aggressive dictator López had a very large army and wished to expand his territories. Independently all prepared for war, Argentina, Brazil, and Uruguay were able to stop Paraguay's powerful military's early advances and in time were able to defeat Paraguay by their combined efforts. By the time the war was over, more than half of the population of Paraguay had perished, including most of its young men making it proportionally the most horrendous and destructive war in South American history.

It was into this war that Gauchito Gil ventured. Naturally he joined the Argentinian Cavalry where his skills as a horseman were much favoured. He was in the forces which repulsed the invasion of Argentina's northern province of Correntes and then at the bloody battle of Tuyutí which is in Paraguay just over the border, about a year later. My father was also at this battle. He was only a Capitán then but he and his engineers were charged with building a temporary road through the marshes and lagoons in front of the Paraguayan defences - the word 'Tuyutí means 'white mud' in the language of the local Guarani people. Here he witnessed the charges of our cavalry of which Trooper Gil was undoubtedly a member. He said that their charges were magnificent. The Paraguayan infantry was on the high ground beyond the marshes and our cavalry swept up the ridge towards them. Their sabres flashed in the sunlight. The sounds of the hooves of their horses sounded like thunder across the pampas. The line of infantry ran to form a defensive square and then the horsemen were upon them. The volleys of the infantry felled many a horse and rider and the sound of sabre upon bayonet rang down to my father who saw it all. One horseman was able to jump over the line and into the square but was dragged from his horse and bayoneted. After a brief struggle the line held and our gallant horsemen were forced to withdraw. They regrouped and charged again. Again they were repulsed. Again they charged and again they were forced to withdraw with heavy losses. The Paraguayans too, had suffered. The ranks of their square were cut in many places. Dead and dying men and horses lay in small heaps across the hill. The infantry clustered together and then were formed back into line by those officers who had survived the charges. The remains of our cavalry were driven off by a regiment of cavalry from the Paraguayan lines. It was a day of slaughter, my father said. Afterward, my father said that the Paraguayans lost over thirteen thousand men killed or captured and our losses were only several hundred. That was dreadful carnage. War cannot be described in terms of the numbers of casualties only, for there are many who also suffered who are not listed as casualties of war.

Gil was one of these. He had received only minor wounds in his charges against the Paraguayans but he had been horrified by the great slaughter which he had witnessed. He had seen the futility of war with the suffering and disgust which was hidden by their initial euphoric feelings of honour and glory. With the war over, he returned to his home in Corrientes Province. Here he was treated as a hero of the war by the local people for he preached peace and the brotherhood of Mankind. Unfortunately this was not a time of peace in Argentina. Civil war had again broken out between the moderate Colorado Party and the Celestes, those who wished for a unified government based in Buenos Aires. When Gil tried to return to his village, he was captured and made to enlist to fight against the Colorado Party. He had had enough of war. He appealed to his captors to relent and make peace with their fellow Argentinians. For this he was considered a deserter and a coward but he was taken never-the-less.

Now here is where the legend of Gauchito Gil starts! No one can say for sure what happened next. Some say that Gil and the other 'volunteers' were locked up in a storehouse whilst the recruiting team went to a nearby cantina for wine. Gil often carried a knife in his boot and it is possible that he used this to free the lock of the storehouse so that he and his companions could escape. When they did so, most ran off to go to their homes and family but two, also gauchos, stayed with Gil to steal the horses of the recruiters to gallop off into the pampas.

Here they soon gathered like-minded men, and some women, who had been driven away from their homes by the warring factions looking for recruits or plunder. Some fled oppression by wealthy estancieros[18] while others simply wanted a life of adventure. Whatever their reason, they were attracted to the doctrines of peace and companionship offered by Gil in a time of civil war and self-protection. Out on the pampas, the group were safe. They knew the local land well and sometimes had the protection of the local gauchos who saw them as their own people. Whenever they found someone deserving their help, they would steal cattle from an estancia or raid a storehouse to give to the oppressed. Gil became adored by the poor people of the pampas who saw him

[18] Owners of the estancias or cattle ranches who were often a law unto themselves.

as an honest thief with a kind heart who advocated peace and love for all, especially those in need.

Of course in such volatile times, such ideals could not be tolerated by the authorities, so they became determined to hunt him down. There are many versions of the story of Gil's capture and death. One says that he was captured whilst at a fiesta to honour St Baltasar because he was betrayed by a friend, but I find that difficult to believe considering the love that the people had for Gil. Others say that he was ambushed by the authorities on his way to the fiesta at Mercedes, and this is the story which I would like to believe. Anyway, he was taken.

What happened next is also open to question but the end result was the same. He was to be taken to the courthouse at the town of Goya which is about fifty kilometres west of Mercedes. Along the way he was murdered. Some say that he was shot by the troops whilst trying to escape. This would be a weak ending for such a man. Several myths say that the Sargento of the troop hated Gil. Perhaps the Sargento was related to those of Gil's past, the brothers of Dona Estrella. Who can tell? It is said that they hung the poor gauchito upside down from a carob tree like they do to beasts which they have slaughtered. Some say they did this to avoid his gaze when they cut his throat. Whichever was the form of his death, one part of the story always comes out. It is always said that before his death, the gauchito told his executioner that he was a man free of sin and that he would forgive him. Furthermore he said that the Sargento's son lay at home dying and that once in Heaven he would intercede on his behalf. The Sargento, a tough veteran of many wars scoffed at this and slit Gil's throat.

Having done his duty and rid the world of the thief Gil, the Sargento continued on with his men to Goya. When he arrived he found that Gaucho Gil had been pardoned of his crimes and would have been freed had he not been executed. The Sargento went to his house and found that his son was indeed on the brink of death. He prayed to Gaucho Gil for aid, and soon as if by a miracle, his son fully recovered. This filled him with much remorse both in being overzealous and killing an innocent men as well as disbelieving Gil's prophesy. In shame and in appreciation for what he believed the spirit of Gil had done, the Sargento went back to the site of the murder and found that the body had been removed for burial. He erected a cross in the ground that had been reddened by Gaucho Gil's blood and later returned with a small statue made in Gil's likeness – a gaucho in a blue shirt and cream trousers, red neckerchief and holding his bolos in his right hand. He placed this statue in front of the cross and the devotion to Gaucho Gil began. Who knows? Perhaps one day he may be made a saint.

Well, Señor Colonel, did you like my stories from the county of my birth?"

"I did. Most interesting, especially to a philosopher! And I am also glad that we have had the opportunity to talk in such an amenable manner. But tell me, how did you come to be in the army of Ecuador?"

"Ah. As you can imagine, Argentinian politics are as fickle as some young women. In 1880, General Roca became President. He and father had always been enemies and father had also been an opponent of the estancieros who had been exterminating the local indigenous peoples. So it was with considerable regret that father thought it expedient to resign his commission and leave Ushuaia. It was a great disappointment to me as I had made many friends there. We were fortunate that a steamer had arrived and that we were able to secure a passage on board her. She continued west along the Beagle Channel and then turned north along the Chilean coast. As Chile and Peru were still too close to the control of the Argentine government across their borders we continued on to the port of Guayaquil in Ecuador. We settled near there and eventually I took citizenship and followed father's wishes and joined the Ecuadoran army as a cadet.

So, there you have it! - The short life of Teniente Gabriel Rivera Peña and his tales from the end of the world.

El octava carta - el simplón de Yanahuara
(The eighth letter - the simpleton of Yanahuara)

This morning I strolled down to the courtyard smoking one of the Comandate's good cigars. I was in a particularly good mood after a good breakfast of sweet buttered rolls, jam, juice and the usual fine coffee. Emerging into the sunlight of the wide courtyard which was in the front part of the hacienda, I saw Garcia sitting on our usual bench.

It was going to be a good day; the air was clear and the sunlight was shining brightly on the red dirt of the outer courtyard. I offered Garcia another cigar and we sat enjoying the fragrance of the tobacco. It was early morning and our peace was interrupted by the opening of both of the double doors of the hacienda. Through it passed a small cart. It was a simple vehicle with plain, homemade wheels and plain wooden sides. It was the cart which had come from the village bring fresh fruit and vegetables for the staff of the hacienda. On the seat of the cart were two men. An old man with grey whiskers, a faded black hat made of old felt and a brown poncho. Next to him slouched a young man, hatless, his hair a lank brown which hung loosely down his face. The cart stopped outside the door to the kitchen allowing the young man to slowly climb down.

"Ah, look Colonel, the youngster is a simpleton." Garcia pointed out.

I watched the young man in question help the older man down from the cart and arm in arm shuffled to its rear to fetch the baskets of produce.

"Yes, Garcia. I think that you are right." I replied.

"What a shame, Señor. To have such a burden to live with." Garcia lamented with some compassion.

"That may be true for some people" I replied, "especially for those who feel that it is because of their own sins. They feel that they must wear their child's affliction like a hair coat and suffer with it. Many people, however learn to live with the situation and eventually see that such people – whom we call simpletons and other names – also have a place in this world. It is said that they are the Children of God and through them we can see God's heart."

"Perhaps you are right, Don Hernán." The simple soldier said looking at me with earnest.

"Perhaps" I replied. "But then I am a philosopher and all philosophers are like storekeepers – they weigh everything and think too much about what the world should be like rather than what it is. I believe that having spent all of our younger years trying to be men - acceptable to others - we lose all of those good virtues which we had as children. Love for all of those around us. Faith in what we are told. Care and helpfulness to all who are in need and of course, our innocence. By that I mean our innocence in thought by looking at everything simply and sometimes finding uncomplicated solutions to our problems. I believe that people like the young man yonder still see the world like a small child. They give love and tenderness without reservation or shame. Look at the way he helps the old man. Perhaps he is his father or grandfather but he shows his love for the man by his assistance."

Garcia looked at the pair with understanding and saw two men not a simpleton and an old man.

I continued. "These two remind me of a story which I was told, a long time ago. It certainly changed my outlook towards such men. Would you like to hear it, Garcia?"

"Si, mi Colonel." He replied with a smile. "I always like to listen to your stories. A rough soldier like myself with very little education has a lot he can learn by such stories."

There was no hint of sarcasm in his voice for I respected Garcia as a simple man with a poor education, other than that which he earned in becoming a professional soldier. In turn, I knew that he respected my learning and travels and easily forgave my shortcomings as a soldier.

"Well then, Garcia. I continued. "This is a story of the simpleton of Yanahuara[1]. It was told to me by the Sacristan of the Church of Saint John the Baptist at Arequipa, the second city of Peru. I do not think that you have been there, as it is on the western side of the Andes east of Puno about two days travel. It is at about two and a half thousand metres above sea level.

[1] This is the Spanish equivalent of the indigenous name Yanawara.

It is a beautiful city within sight of three active volcanoes; the rugged shapes of Pichu Pichu, Chachani and the mighty cone of El Misti. The city is built on the slopes of Misti and the river Chili comes down off its slopes. All of our country's western slopes of the Andes are deserts and it is only because of rivers like this that such cities can survive. The city is mostly made of fine stone with cobbled streets and a large Plaza de Armes with a large cathedral on one side and the government buildings on the other. Joining the two on each side of the plaza are colonnaded buildings which house a number of shops. The authorities in Arequipa are proud of their city and call it the 'White City' because the beautiful buildings are made from the fine white volcanic rock from the mountains. However some say that this name is used in jest by the early indigenous people to mean that it is the city where the white people, that is the Spaniards, lived.

The barrio where I stayed was called 'Yanahuara' after the tribe who lived in the region. Their name 'Yanawara' possibly is Quechua for 'those who wear black short trousers'."

Garcia grinned at that for he spoke Quechua as his native tongue, although a northern dialect of it, and he replied. "Black shorts! That would be interesting to see."

"Well." I continued. "It would be what they were used to. Our Andean peoples wear many different types of costume as you well know and we can often tell from which village they come, by their dress. It may be a head covering, shawl or trousers but that is what they are happy in. You know, on the isle of

Taquile in Lake Titicaca where the men do the knitting, the women know which men are available for marriage by the colour and form of their soft caps - it identifies his relationship status. If a cap is coloured red and white it means he is single, red and blue means he is engaged and all red means he is married. Furthermore, the direction of the extended top is the way to express a man's current state of mind. If the top is laid to the right side, it means he is happy and content. Left side indicates he's worrying about something and wants to keep the problems away. The most common, especially when they are knitting, is the hat top to the back. This means they are busy.

Well then, to my story. I had gone to Arequipa for some reason or another to do with my civilian occupation as a teacher. Perhaps it was a conference or lecture. I do not recall. I stayed in a small posada in the district of Yanahua, which is to the northwest of the Plaza de Armes, and went to Mass at the Church of Saint John the Baptist which was nearby. This is a beautiful church built over one hundred years ago also of the fine, white stone of the mountains. It has a good square tower and the portico is finely decorated. Here I met the old Sacristan and we became good friends over the short time of my stay. Perhaps he was sympathetic to my philosophical nature or perhaps it was that he had a good story to tell to a newcomer, I do not know, but he told me a story which showed the nature of one such Child of God. This is his story"

"I am an old man now but in my youth I also attended this church. I was a choirboy and went to the little school behind the building run by the good Sisters. At this time there was a poor labourer who worked for the church and lived in a small hovel just down the hill. As you see, the church is built on a high ridge which runs down to the terraced fields built by the Old People.

Now this man had a son called Juan who was a simpleton. He went to our school but the Sisters found him a very difficult student. Oh, it was not because he was a bad child. Far from it! He was quiet and gentle in nature and always had a big smile. Sister Amelia was always upset at this. She would come into the classroom and Juan would be leaning on his desk with his mouth open in this idiotic smile and saliva drooling out of the corner of his mouth.

'Ugh, Juan! Close your mouth.' She would say, and we would all laugh. Juan would laugh too, as it was not in his nature to take offence. We would call him 'Loco Juan' or 'el tonto[2]' behind his back. Some of the more rowdy children would often play tricks on him but he just smiled and would quietly go about his business. Children can be very cruel at times.

His mother had died when he was in his infancy – perhaps she could not bear the thought of having a simpleton – but his father loved him dearly and would do his best to give his only son a good life. The good Sisters tried too, but their attempts to teach him his letters simply went astray. Eventually he left our small school and helped his father in his small

[2] 'The fool'

tasks of maintaining the church. Sometimes he would take his small cart around the streets carrying whatever he could for the older people and the lame as well as picking up any discarded item which might be of value. Sometimes he would go down the hill and help the farmers cultivate their corn and potatoes in the old terraced gardens.

Juan was not a big lad like most of his former classmates. He was thin and not very tall. His skin eventually was burnt to the hard brown colour of the labourer and his sparse hair hung down, long and untidy. One thing that his father was able to teach his son was a love of music. In the evenings when their work for the day had been done, they would sit on the edge of the ridge and the old man would teach his son to play the guitar and sing some of the old songs of the Yanawara people. Some unkind souls would say that in both these two things the old man failed. Oh, Juan could play the guitar and sing but neither was harmonious or with any gusto. But Juan and the old man were happy and lived quietly in their small house near the church.

When the old man died – Juan would have been aged about thirty as we are of a similar age – Juan was distraught and mourned him for a long time. The priest saw to it that the old man had a good funeral and the good Sisters did all they could for poor Loco Juan. One of the wealthier parishioners who had appreciated the old man's help paid for a small vault in the long panel of raised vaults which are the custom here as the ground is very hard. Is it not the same in your city, Señor?"

"Yes" I replied. It is our custom also. In the mountains there is very little soil to waste on cementarios so we also have rows of vaults stacked four or five on top of each other and in a long line."

"I think that they are better than the ugly graves which are dug into the ground." He continued. "In front of the small wall in front of the coffin and behind a nice sheet of glass we can put small mementos of the departed and perhaps a small likeness. Juan's father's window had a small guitar and some small flowers made from cloth which one of the good Sisters found in the church.

So Loco John continued his father's work – he had no other skills – but he was a different character to his father. He would pull his little cart around the streets singing his strange little songs but always he had a big grin and a cheerful

'Hola!' to all he passed. The dogs in the streets would come to him with their tails all wagging and it often seemed that the birds in the sky would sing with him. By now, the rest of us boys had also grown up and were too intent with learning the skills of Manhood to pay much attention to Juan. Oh, there were a few who would still shout abuse at him to enlarge their own feelings of self-importance, but most people were kind to Loco Juan. He became part of the local scenery. He would come down the same street at about the same time and help all those who needed him. He would carry some of the baskets of the womenfolk who went down the hill to barter for vegetables from the farmers on the terraces. He would help anyone who needed a hand. He never asked for any money but was always thankful when someone gave him a few coins or some food in exchange for his labours. On Saturdays, Juan would leave his little cart at home and wander through the streets with his battered old guitar. He would sing his funny songs but in a soft voice so as not to disturb anyone. Sometimes people would come to their gate and wish him well and he did not mind his name of 'Loco Juan'. He would return their salutes with a cheerful 'buenas dias' and continue on his way.

In the afternoon, he would take his little cart out of the barrio and up the road which lead to the local refuse mound. Here he would look for anything of value which he might sell to the traders along the street of the Puente[3] Bolagnesi which crosses the Chili and goes up the hill to

[3] Bridge

the Plaza de Armes in the centre of the city.

Of all of the items which Loco Juan scavenged from the refuse mound, his most prized items where the old bottles which had been discarded over the centuries. He rarely sold those but kept them on shelves along the wall of his shack. I know, because when I became the new Sacristan – I was much younger then – I went with Father Bartholomew one day to offer some pastoral care, we saw Juan's fine collection of old bottles. He would sometimes pass by an antique shop with one of his latest finds and ask the opinion of the owner. As everyone liked Loco Juan he would get an honest reply and sometimes an offer to buy, but he rarely sold.

Now Fate often leads Man along unexpected paths. One day Juan went off his usual route and down a street which led to a wealthier part of the city. Here were some grand houses which were from the colonial times. They had large front gates and gardens which were overlooked by beautiful balconies. Juan wandered down this street singing his quiet song and a few people came out to see who it was. Some smiled and wished him a good day but others went back inside or closed their shutters. At one large and imposing house a lady saw Juan passing and called for him to wait. Soon a maid came out and offered Juan a cool drink. This was something new to Juan and the lady was the most beautiful woman that he had ever seen. He was entranced. After that day he would regularly wander down that street, hoping that he would see the beautiful lady again.

This lady was Señora Elena Medina Campos, the wife of Coronel Fernando Medina Montero, a most disagreeable man. He was despised by his troops for his aggressive character and poor leadership and by his peers for his arrogance. It was difficult to believe that such a beautiful woman, both in appearance and spirit would marry such a man. Perhaps he may have been a dashing officer in his youth or perhaps the marriage had been arranged. Who knows?

Whatever the reason, Doña Elena was loved by all she met. She was always there if a friend or neighbour needed help and she always had a smile on her beautiful face. No problem was too great a burden for her to solve with a laugh and a smile. Perhaps she felt sorry for poor Loco Juan and that is why she often would send her maid down to the gate to offer him a cool drink if it was warm or an extra coat if it was cold. Anyway, Juan became a regular visitor to that street and the others in the neighbourhood soon became at least tolerant of his poor guitar playing and raucous songs.

No-one really knows what happened on that fateful day. Some say that Doña Elena was at the gate farewelling her husband who was going to his regiment when Loco Juan came down the street. Don Fernando did not like Juan and all of those who were not to his standard of perfection. He reined his horse around to push the simpleton away with Doña Elena still clutching his saddle. The Colonel beat his wife with his riding crop and brave Juan tried to stop him but was caught unawares and fell beneath the hooves of the Colonel's horse. The

Colonel continued to trample the horse over the poor man and in desperation, Doña Elena pulled the pistol out of the Colonel's holster with both hands pleading with her husband to stop. Alas, the pistol discharged and the Colonel fell from his horse which bolted down the street.

At the sound of the gunshot, many people ran into the street. Doña Elena had crumpled to the ground to console her dying husband but the simpleton lay still on the cobbles. Someone sent for a doctor and a priest but only the priest was needed. Father Bartholomew came quickly and gave the last rites to the Colonel and Juan whilst Doña Elena's maid took her into the house. The Colonel's body was carried into the house by his servants and Juan's body was placed carefully onto his little cart by some of the men who had run into the street. With the help of some of these men, Father Bartholomew wheeled the little cart containing Loco Juan's body back to his little hovel down the hill from the church.

The Colonel was later buried by his regiment's Chaplain in a quiet ceremony with only Doña Elena, her maid and a few officers who were there out of duty rather than compassion for their colleague. Juan had had a more elaborate ceremony at this church with many people from Yanahuara coming to pay their respects. Some money was raised and Juan's body was interred in a vault above the ground not far that of his father. In the glass front of the vault they put a small wooden model of a cart, a guitar and several small painted flowers made of wood which the children had carved. You can see his vault over there Señor. It is never without flowers in the vases at the front of the vault."

"And what happened to the poor wife, Doña Elena?" I replied.

"Ah" said the Sacristan. "That is the only good which came from this sad event. She sold all of her possessions and gave the money to the poor of the city. She took her maid and entered into the Monasterio de Santa Catalina[4] not far from the Cathedral and the Plaza de Armes. From here she was able to visit many of the sick and poor of the city in honour of poor Loco Juan and in

[4] The Monastery of Saint Catherine was founded in 1580 by a rich widow, Doña María de Guzmán. The nuns are of the Dominican Second Order and those pious young ladies who were admitted were of the upper classes who were house in good quarters and were allowed to take some servants with them. The Monastery today is more of a tourist attraction.

penitence for the death of her husband. She became very well known for her good works and the people called her 'La Doña Blanca[5]'.

So then! That is my story of Loco Juan of Yanahuara. Poor John was a simpleton to be sure, but he was greatly loved for his infectious happy innocence, his helpfulness and his final act of bravery."

Having finished my account of the Sacristan's story, I turned and looked at the young simpleton helping the old man with his cartload of vegetables. "So what do you see there?" I said to Garcia.

"Now I see a man helping another not a simpleton anymore." He replied.

"Yes Garcia." I continued. "We are all of God's children but some, like that man

5 The White Lady.

and poor Loco Juan continue to be full of His grace, even when the rest of us having grown to Manhood have lost many of the virtues which He gave us. In many ways it is sad that we are not more like the simpleton of Yanahuara."

El noveno carta – el camino a la Buena Esperanza

(The ninth letter - the road to Good Hope)

He was sitting slumped forward with his head in his hands. This was unusual for the brave Sargento who always held himself erect and had a very positive outlook on life in general.

"Hola, Garcia! How are you this morning?" I said sitting beside him. At my voice he sat up in surprise and resumed the role of the tough soldier.

"Buenos dias, Colonel. I am fine thank you," he lied.

"Oh Garcia," I replied putting my arm around his broad shoulders. "I know you too well. We are friends too, are we not?

There is something bothering you, I can tell."

I had lived in the high Andes all of my life and had spent many years with the true Andinos of my mother's family. It is said that the people of the mountains can feel impending doom and often go into a state of acceptance, becoming morose and sullen.

Garcia look up and quietly said "You are right, Don Hernán. I feel as if we will never leave this place. I feel that I will never see my wife and children again. Do you not feel it too? The blood of the Andes run in your veins also."

"Yes, Garcia." I replied. "There are times when I too feel depressed but there is nothing much that I can do about it so I look in another direction. It is better to look for hope rather than hopelessness. A wise traveler looks through the trees for his cottage rather than trying to see the whole forest. With that, I could see that my homespun philosophy was lost on Garcia who is a practical man in all thoughts and deeds.

"Look!" I continued. I will tell you a story of hope. It is a story of my childhood. Me, Hernán Morano. At a time when all was lost and there was very little hope in the world. It is a personal story which will have many things in it of which you would be familiar. But listen! Listen to the thoughts behind the words rather than the places and customs which you would probably know well.

As you may know, I was brought up in a well-to-do family in Cuzco. My father was a lawyer and a lesser politician of a progressive party. We lived in a big house and had many servants. My mother was descended from a royal line of the Incas and she had many brothers who lived in the country not far from the city and also in Puno on Lake Titicaca. I was a happy but only child of the family. This all came to an end when I was about six. My father suddenly died. It was his heart, the doctors said. My mother took his loss very badly and I remember much weeping and mourning. I felt the loss greatly because I thought that Mother would die also and that I would be alone. This was my greatest fear; even though my Uncle Eduardo had promised to look after me should that happen. He was a very clever man and knew people well. Perhaps he knew what my fears were. Also, when he died, father had left many debts and we had difficulty living on the small amount which he had left us. Many of our servants were dismissed with great sorrow for they had looked after us for years. Our house became a dark place with drawn curtains and my mother dressed in black. Life was full of hopelessness and the future was one of continued gloom.

One day, about a year after my father's death, Mother received a letter from her Aunt Isabella who lived out in the country not far from the little village of Checacupe on the highway to Puno about ninety kilometres south of Cuzco. She had moved there when she married a local farmer and they lived together a few kilometres out of the village on a road called el camino a la Buena Esperanza – the road to Good Hope. It had been named by some of the earliest Spanish settlers there who thought that there might have been gold in the mountains nearby. The gold was not there and the Spanish later moved on leaving the country to the local people who farmed the dry land. By all accounts, my mother's Uncle Guillermo was well-to-do. Their farm backed onto the Urubamba River which flows from the mountains southeast of Cuzco and then for hundreds of miles along the valleys of the Andes until it reaches the Tambo River and then into the mighty Amazon."

"Yes!" Garcia exclaimed. "I remember this river and its valley. It was only a few years ago when my Company marched along the road which followed the river. We marched south to stop the invasion of our country from Chile but we only got as far as Pucara."

"That is right, Garcia." I continued. Pucara is only about one hundred and fifty kilometres further south from there.

I had to march that distance myself when my Regiment marched south. Such a good thing too, as that is where we met, remember?"

"Ah, si mi Colonel." He replied with a grin. "That was a good day, but I do not remember much about the march except that it was a long one and took us over a week to get there. It was fortunate that there was a good road and that there was not much climbing and with plenty of water nearby."

"Well, then." I continued. "To get back to my story, my mother had received this invitation. I am sure now that one of my uncles would have let Doña Isabella know of my mother's sad loss for they were a close family. You know, after my father's death, we did not see much of his family. He had a brother who visited us once but he seemed to be very distant from my father and there was no more contact which I can remember. Later my mother mentioned briefly that this uncle was of very humble circumstance and had moved away to another part of Peru with his family. That was a pity, for I found that my mother's brothers were a great comfort to us after my father's death and became even closer."

"Uncles are good people." Garcia said with a laugh. "I had many uncles – some not even related to by mother and father. As children we called all adults who were friends of the family 'uncle'. It was the custom in our part of the northern mountains, but Mother also had five brothers and two sisters and my father a similar number, so we were not short of family, you understand."

"You are right, there." I said." Family is important. I only regret that I was the only child in mine. My father was much older than my mother and he always seemed to be busy trying to solve the problems of our country; he would often go on long political campaigns for his party but achieved very little.

Well then, my mother decided to go to Aunt Isabella for a short stay. This was exciting! I had never been out of Cuzco before and only knew the streets of my local barrio and my few friends who lived nearby. I had never been to the country before but my uncles, especially Uncle Eduardo had told me stories of life in the country when they all lived as a family near Checacupe. I remember our day of departure well. Even after all of those years. It started with the gloomy rays of the morning sun just before dawn, creeping like some clammy finger along the corridor of our house and into our bedroom. My mother had moved my little bed into her bedroom at the front of our house for she felt very alone without my father and she too, may have been apprehensive of losing the only other member of her family.

'Is it time to get up, Mama?' I called in the gloom.

'No, not yet Hernán' She eventually replied.

I repeated this question several times as the light became brighter and I feared that we would miss the start of our adventure.

We had a very light breakfast and our last manservant, Julio, took our bags outside and went to get our small carriage. It was quite through the streets of Cuzco at that early hour in the morning. We passed by the Plaza de

Armes which was once the Haukaypata –
the Great Square of the Incas. Today
there stands a fountain and the statue of
Pachacuti, the ninth Inca who was
responsible for the expansion of the
Incan Empire. We drove downhill along
the Avenida el Sol which runs into the
Avenida San Martin on which the posada
which acts as the main coaching station
stood. Here was much excitement for a
small child. There were many people
here waiting to take their coach to some
distant place. There were porters who
took the bags for each of the coaches
which would leave from here and there
were many people selling food and last-
minute items to the passengers. I sat
quietly on a small bench whilst my
mother went to pay the departure tax at
the little kiosk outside the archway of the
posada. After a short while we were
called to board the coach for Puno. The

driver, a big man with huge mustachios, a red shirt with a thick neckerchief saw me and asked my mother if I would like to see the horses. He took me to the front of the stage where there were four horses harnessed to the coach. They were huge! Not like the small pony which Julio had with our town carriage. These horses were magnificent. They were well kept; their coats were all of a uniform brown colour and their mains had been carefully plaited. They stood there patiently, occasionally snorting and pawing the dirt with their hooves. They were ready to go and so was I.

Because we were only going part of the way, we climbed up into the cab and settled ourselves in the seats facing the direction we were to travel. There were four other passengers who paid their respects to my widowed mother and then went about their own business; one reading a newspaper and the rest generally looking out of the windows waiting for us to start our journey.

Suddenly we were off! A shout from the driver and the coach started with a sudden lurch. Down the cobbled street we went. The people of the streets waved their hats and gave us a cheer for good luck. What adventure! For ages it seemed that we clattered through the tall buildings of the city and passed the other carriages and carts which also shared our thoroughfare. Eventually the clatter on the cobbles ceased and we were on the dirt of the highway leaving Cuzco heading south.

We had left the city by now. There were no longer any tall buildings and the throng of people going about their morning affairs. Now we were travelling along a dusty road with wooded hills coming steeply down on each side. The dust of the road came into the coach and the noise of the rattling fittings and the horses' hooves clatter only added to the adventure. Mother coughed because of the dust and put a handkerchief to her mouth. She gladly exchanged seats with me so that I could look out of the window. 'Don't lean out so far, Hernán!' she said and I withdrew my head into the cab. It had been fun to feel the air and the dust on my face!

After a time which passed so quickly for me because of all the things to see along the way, we slowly came to rest at our first coaching stop. This was at a large posada on the banks of a fast-flowing river which flowed north into another valley on our left-hand side. Mother said that this was the village of Huarcapay and the river was the mighty Urubamba River[1] which eventually flows into the mighty Amazon. There was not much here except the posada, a large building of two stories with a large arch to allow the spare horses to exit. Our coach pulled onto the side of the road whilst the horses were changed and we were allowed to alight and stretch our legs. Nearby, some of the local woman had several small tables upon which sat some of their home-made items. They all wore long woven skirts with long pants of a contrasting colour beneath. Some wore red, flat, rounded hats which looked as they were upside down. Mother said that they were called Monteras, which is a Quechua word. These sit only on the top

[1] Its name possibly comes from the Quechua *Willkamayu* for 'sacred river', it starts to the southeast of Cuzco and flows north-north-west for 724 kilometers before joining the Ucayali River and then the Amazon.

of the head and are held there by a thick woven strap called a sanq'apa, which is decorated with a layer of beads, which ties the hat under the chin. The number of beads generally reflects the social status of the woman, but the style and colour of headdress varies according to the region from which they come. Over their shoulders, most of the ladies wore a Lliclla which is a type of cape. A lliclla[2] is usually a square piece of cloth which is secured at the front using a tupu, a sturdy safety pin, or it may be worn tied. These tupus were woven in many bright colours, often in a series of contrasting colours and with motifs of llamas and other animals. But red was the dominant colour here and matched their skirts"

[2] Prononounced [lyiclya i.e. lyeelyah] is a small shoulder shawl, usually brightly colour and often with striped designs and held with a pin called a tupu.

"Si, Si, Patrón" Garcia interrupted. "In my village, the womanfolk wear broader black hats with a wide yellow fringe all around and they have several long skirts we call Polleras which are made from handwoven wool cloth we call bayeta. The women may wear three or four of these in layers. Often the hem of each skirt is lined with a colourful trim called puyto which may also be black."

"Just so." I continued. "The ladies in Huarcapay were also very colourful. The dresses in the streets of Cuzco were more European and sometimes bordering on shabby with the poorer people. Mother was happy here with these women. She smiled and laughed. This was the first time that I had seen her do this since father died. She also conversed freely in Quechua, her native tongue. At home we always spoke only Spanish as Father did not speak Quechua. Mother had taught me her language so I had some idea what they were saying. She spoke to them of little things, mostly about the weather and crops and about their beautiful home-made woven cloth. The ladies were very flattered that such a high-born lady, especially one in mourning would speak to them so fluently in their own language. Mother bought some cloth from them and also a little toy Alpaca made from real fur of that animal. He was very soft and I called him 'Paco'. He was to become my favourite toy.

We climbed back up into the coach and continued our journey. After we joined the valley of the Urubamba, the road followed the river which flowed rapidly in the opposite direction to which we travelled. The river originates on the slopes of Khunurana, which is near the pass at La Raya on the road about one hundred and forty kilometres further south. Mother told me this because that pass is the highest in Peru at over four thousand metres above the sea. We were only going about half the distance to La Raya which meant that the road would only be a gentle climb. After La Raya, the valley gradually widened until it became the vast altiplano which contained the mighty Lake Titicaca and Puno, the coach's final destination.

Indeed, the valley seemed to open up a little but this only made the row of high and snow-covered mountains on both sides of the valley seem even higher and more majestic. I could see why my mother's people often spoke about the apus[3] of the mountains. Down on the

3 Mountain gods.

floor of the valley there were many small farms on the other side of the river. I was fascinated by the way the people lived here. It was so different from the crowded buildings and cobbled streets of Cuzco. Within the midst of the cultivated fields there would be a compound with a high wall of adobe bricks enclosing several small buildings with one often being two stories high. Most were covered in red tiled rooves with a long line of rounded tiles at their peak. Of course most would have the toritos[4] and a crucifix at their centre. Mother told me that the adobe bricks were made of mud and straw which had been dried in the sun."

[4] The Toritos de Pucará are small ceramic bulls, usually in a pair which are brightly painted and placed on the centre of the roof arch for good luck. They are common in the area around the village of Pucara further south and are often placed on the roof next to a crucifix. The story of this has been explained in the Fifth Letter.

"Oh, yes!" Garcia interrupted. "I remember as a teenager helping my uncles made such bricks. It was much fun at the beginning but became hard as we had to make many of them and carry the mud from the edge of the lagoon near the river. I would have to stamp around in a pool of thick mud and my cousin Juanita would laugh at me and throw the chopped straw under my feat. 'Here, Don Muddy-legs' she would taunt as she threw on more straw. But eventually as the wall was built we had a great sense of pride in what the family had done.

"Perhaps that was one of the simple joys of country life, Garcia? In Cuzco, our home was made of cut stone and if part of it fell down, my father had to wait until a mason could be found. And then it cost a lot of money. There must be a great sense of community to build your own home with the help of your family and neighbours.

Well, to continue my story – and I have no doubt that the countryside south of Cuzco in the valley of the Urubamba would have scenes which you would be familiar with, but as a small boy every little thing here was new, and everything was a great delight. From the coach window I could see the country folk going about their daily chores: a man in a black cloak walking along leading his cow; a woman in a brown hat carrying a load on her back in her brightly-coloured k'eperina[5]; men and women working together in their fields of potatoes, maize tall and green and fluffy rows of quinoa. Occasionally we would pass by a small village. These would consist of a small

[5] This is a large rectangular carrying cloth worn over the back and knotted in front. Children and goods are securely held inside.

cluster of adobe houses and possibly a small church with its square tower rising above the rooves of the houses.

We had several other short stops to change the horses and give us some relief from the jolting of the coach but just as the sun was setting behind the distant mountains we arrived at the village of Checacupe. It was like most of the other villages which we had passed but only a little bigger. Many of the houses clustered near the road were of two stories with arched doors and windows on the lowest story. All were made of the brown adobe bricks, giving the village a uniform drab appearance in the fading light. At least the posada, which was also the coaching stop seemed to have some life about it with a cheerful light in several of the windows. The owner was ready to greet the passengers as this would be their stop for the night.

We alighted, cramped and tired from our long journey. The dust of the road had settled over us and my mother wiped some of the red dust from my face with her handkerchief. Our bags had been taken from the rear of the coach and placed on the ground next to the wall of the posada. When the coach and its horses were led through the archway and into the courtyard, I could see across the road that there was a great lake stretching across to the rounded hills beyond. The water looked black in the poor light and the edges of the lake were ringed by many high tuffs of reeds and grass.

'That is Laguna Pomacanchi' said our driver, a smile on his broad weather-beaten face. 'I hope that you are not kept waiting for your family.' Indeed, he was right for a small, broad-shouldered man approached us and took off his broad sombrero. 'Dona Valentina?' he addressed my mother. When my mother gave him a smile he continued. 'Buenas tardes[6], I am your cousin Ramone. I will take you to Dona Isabella'. With that he took up our bags in each hand and led the way to a small cart with a donkey tethered to a small post. He threw the bags onto the back of the cart and helped my mother climb up onto the front seat. 'Would the boy like to ride with us or sit in the back?' He asked my mother. I did not wait for the reply but climbed up over the side of the cart and settled myself against the back of the seats. I was enjoying all of this and to ride in a small

[6] 'Good afternoon'

cart was great fun, lying back and looking up at the stars in the clear, black sky. They were so bright. Much brighter than in Cuzco where the cooking fires and those of the factories often made the sky very dull.

We crossed a small stone bridge which crossed the gurgling Urubamba which at this place, was only about twenty metres wide, but very fast flowing. We then turned onto a small road which followed the river south and upstream. We passed a small, weathered signpost which simply said 'Buena Esperanza' – Good Hope. I turned to Ramone and asked him why the road was given that name. He responded 'We are not sure Cousin Hernán, but we think that the Spaniards were looking for gold up there in the mountains and that this was the road they built to their mine. Perhaps there may be gold up there or perhaps not. Anyway, the Spaniards have gone now and there is nothing to mark the site. I know. As a boy my friends and I explored the end of the road but there was nothing there, just some flat hollows in the side of the mountain and a few old pieces of iron. No gold.' I thanked Ramone for his story. Perhaps I would also go looking for gold. It is said that these mountains have many metals of value.

After what seemed to be a short time we came to a wall which had two large wooden doors. They were painted green and one of them was open. There was a bright lantern hanging from a large hook on one of its side posts. Mother climbed down from the seat assisted by Cousin Ramone as I eagerly jumped down from the cart. Little Margarita – for that was the donkey's name – shuffled a little but then resumed her docile stance.

'Buenas noches[7] - welcome, welcome'! The warm, friendly voice came from a stout old lady standing just inside the gate. She had the leggings and coloured skirts which I had seen on many of the womenfolk along the way. She had a thick red shawl around her head and shoulders. She embraced my mother with a big hug and then turned to me also saying, 'This must be little Hernán, Oh how thin and pale you look. We will have to get you working with the other boys'.

Garcia laughed at this reference to his Colonel.

---

[7] 'good evening' or 'good night' even though it is plural and literally means 'good nights.'

'Come in. Come in. Ramone – bring the bags. Oh, my little ones you must be very tired after your long trip. Come in,' she said, leading the way into the compound with a small building just inside. We went through a very low door into a room full of warmth and light. On a broad wooden table scrubbed white was a modern pressure lamp similar to the one we had at home. Opposite the door in the wall of the room, which was also part of the wall surrounding the compound, was a small fireplace in which a bright fire of wood crackled. One end of the room contained the table and several chairs whilst the other end had a small stove made of clay sitting up against the wall. This was a simple hollow box of clay about fifty centimetres long and about thirty high. It had an opening in the front for making the fire and two small holes on its top on which were placed two stone pots. We had pots at home too, but nothing like these. Our kitchen pots were European and usually made from iron but these were made from baked red clay. They were both very round and squat. One of them looked like an ordinary pot with a wide, round opening at the top which was covered by a round lid with a small knob on top. The other pot was unlike any which I had seen before – not that I had had much knowledge of kitchen pottery, even our own. This pot had a large oval opening with a flattened bottom looking somewhat like a wide, sad grimace. Like the ones which I had seen on posters for the comedy theatres in Cuzco with a happy face and a sad face. On top of the pot was a handle for lifting. There were a few glowing embers in the interior of the stove suggesting that a warm meal might be nearby.

Yes! There it was. On the table were two plates completely covered with food. There were potatoes of several kinds; some peeled and some with black and red skins, corn cobs with several colours of kernel, peppers, beans and some small pieces of chopped cheese. There was also a jug of juice on the table. This was of a clear colour and thick. It tasted good but different to anything which I had tasted before. It was the juice of the aloe plant which grows all over the mountains.

'Please, sit and eat for I am sure that you both must be hungry.' Doña Isabella said.' After you have eaten, I will take you up to your room and you can get a good night's sleep'

Ramone appeared in the doorway and bade us a 'good night' and went out to continue his journey back to his farm. Having eaten, Doña Isabella led the way up the stairway which was on the outside of the house to an upper room. We entered through a very low door for which Mother had to bend, being somewhat taller than most women. In the room was a large double bed with tall brass-topped corner posts and a brightly coloured bedspread made from woven alpaca wool. It had many different coloured stripes, mostly red and pink with some of them having little figures in blue woven within their borders. Above the bedhead was a large crucifix and a large candle burnt brightly on a side table. At the other end of the bed was a large chest-of-drawers with a wash bowl and water jug made out of fine pottery which had been lacquered white and blue. Our bags were sitting on the floor near the side of the bed.

'Allin tuta[8], my dears.' Doña Isabella said with a warm smile. 'Sleep well'. She looked up at my mother and said. If you want to go during the night, use the pot under the bed. I will show you where everything is in the morning.' Mother unpacked the bags quickly and found my nightshirt and I climbed into the large, soft bed and was soon fast asleep.

The next day began with a strong, clear light coming through the two little windows of our room. I could see now that the walls were painted in a light pastel blue colour which I had not noticed the night before. I had slept late because the bed was very comfortable and I had been very tired. The mattress was made with alpaca wool and the sheets were of fine cotton. Mother was

8 'Good night' in Quechua

not there, so I found my dressing gown which was hanging on one of the bedposts and went out onto the small balcony which ran the length of the building. This I noticed was in the shape of a large' L' with three doors opening out onto the balcony which followed around the outside of the building. The stairway which we had come up the night before was in the middle of this balcony. It had been made of brick also and had its own railing of iron. The steps were broad as I had remembered but I had not seen the faded letters which had once been written in red on the front of each of three steps. The words were in Quechua which my mother had taught me and read: 'Ama Sua; Ama Llulla; and Ama Quella[9]. This I was later told was the creed of the Inca. At the foot of the

[9] 'Don't Lie; Don't steal; Don't be lazy'

stairs, in a small recess within the tiled floor and covered over by strong glass were several small earthenware bowls containing some dried potatoes, some dried corn and some seeds which I could not identify. These were explained as an offering to Pachamama, the earth goddess to care for the people within the house.

I looked around the compound which was formed by this large building, a high adobe wall, the small, single story kitchen building and another of similar size over on the other wall facing the stairway. Below the floor was beautifully tiled with a bare section on one side of the main building which led to the stables and storeroom below. There was the main gateway with its large, green doors and a small archway over the top and another small doorway, also painted green just below the stairs.

I went down the stairs and stood in the small courtyard. Below part of the upper balcony was a long ledge which held various pots and jugs and two wash basins. There was also a small well, set over in the corner of the compound with a green lid of wood protecting it from the dust and a small bucket on the end of a coil of rope which hung on the wall nearby.

I looked into the window of the other small building and found that it was a type of storeroom with racks of jars and bundles and several racks containing piles of potatoes, dried corn and other vegetables. In another corner, outside and raised on a small shelf was a large, covered box made out of many separated slates. Curious, I raised the lid and found several guinea pigs scurrying around its floor looking back at me. I had heard that the country people used these as food but in Cuzco we had other meat more common to a European diet. I closed the lid quickly, not knowing whether to feel sorry for these soft little animals or thankful that the people in the mountains were so self-sufficient. I never did like to eat these animals, even though the flesh was said to be very good.

Under the main building were more storage spaces containing large water jars and Doña Isabella's cow which she called Ana who was kept in a small pen. She was milked every day and there was plenty of hay in the store rooms for her and milk, cream and cheese for us.

I found Mother in the kitchen where Doña Isabella was cooking on the little clay stove. She did not use the large fireplace except when much hot water was needed or a large stew was being prepared. There was a big black metal pot for these purposes hanging from a chain from the roof of the fireplace. We were lucky that at this height, which was just over three thousand metres, some small trees could grow and so firewood, though difficult to find was still available. Higher in the mountains, the poor farmers had to make do with dried dung from their llamas and what dried vegetation could be scavenged. Breakfast consisted of banana fritters of fried whole bananas covered with a rich chocolate sauce within a corn cachapa or pancake. With this my mother had some freshly-brewed coffee and I had a little milk.

Later, after further exploration I found that the little green door in the furthest wall led to a cleared pathway lined with white-painted rocks. This went outside for a few metres to a small hut of adobe with a thatched roof which was el inodoro or the toilet.

My exploration of Doña Isabella's farm–or should I now say 'Mamma'[10], for that was what she wanted me to call her – was a great adventure. Unlike home in Cuzco, where the streets could be dangerous even during the day because of the traffic, I was allowed to wander freely around the general area. Her farm was now only quite small because she had given much of her land to her sons who had their own small farms nearby. Her husband of many years, Uncle Guillermo was now mostly bed-ridden and could no longer till the land. He spent most of his time in the main

10 Pronounced [Mam-ah]

bedroom upstairs. He was a kindly old man and I would often visit him or take his dinner up at night. He had built this farm with the help of his brothers over sixty years ago when he was a strong farmer with a new bride. Outside, Mamma still had some small plots of potatoes, corn and other vegetables and had several hens which roamed freely around the tall grass near the walls of the compound. Every Saturday there was a market in Checacupe and her youngest son Ramone would come with his little cart and take us into the village. For less important purchases and especially for Mass on Sundays Mamma, Mother and I would walk the few kilometres along the road, over the little stone bridge and into the village and to the church of the Virgin of Immaculate Conception.

On these trips we would often pass people going to their farms. The men would doff their hats or give a smile and a little bow and say 'Buenos Dias, Doña Isabella'. The womenfolk would also pay courtesy to Mamma. She was obviously a lady of high standing in the area. Uncle Guillermo told me one day when I visited him for one of his stories that his people had fled Cuzco over three hundred years ago when the Spaniards came. They had been minor officials under Huáscar, the son of the Inca Huayna Capac, they had left the capital to settle quietly on the land. As the new Spanish conquest spread, they eventually accepted baptism into the Church and became prosperous land-owners. This continued through to today although Uncle Guillermo had become too old and ill to continue farming so he had given much of his land to his sons. The family had grown of course, so that many of the local farmers were related in some way or other. Uncle Guillermo had met Doña Isabella in Cuzco and had later brought his new bride back to Checacupe where he and his brothers had built this fine new house.

In the village we would visit the many little stalls which would be set up in the wide space at the bend in the road not far from the posada where we had alighted from the coach a few days ago. These were little stalls made of wooden frames with thatched roofs. The ladies at each stall would be in their most colourful dress, they would greet us with a broad smile while showing us what they had for sale. There would be mounds of grains, especially many different coloured corns, potatoes in many different varieties, red, black and cream as well as other vegetables. There would be many handicrafts of leather and wood, brightly woven cloth, hats and caps and small wooden painted toys. Of course there would also be many hand-made icons and statues of Jesus, Mary and the saints and some others which belonged to the old religion. Mother and Mamma would slowly walk along these stalls, talking happily with their owners. Mamma would introduce my mother and me to many of these ladies who would be most courteous to us. One old man who had a stall full of little carvings gave me a little bull from Pucara, brightly painted blue with golden horns.

At other times, Cousin Ramone would bring his family to the house and we would all have an evening meal around the big table in the kitchen. It often would be getting cold in May at that altitude so a fire would be lit and we would have a large spread of food. I would join Cousin Ramone's two smaller children on a special mat in front of the fire and we would have our food there. This was our 'picnic' where we would eat and tell stories with much laughter. At the table, the adults and older children would all do the same. It was good to see my mother laugh again and become fully involved with the conversation about the goings-on of this relative and that relative and so on. After dinner was over, the ladies would clear away all of the dishes and take them outside to be washed in the courtyard bench and Cousin Ramone would go outside and light his smelly old pipe. After this, the adults would go upstairs to the third and largest room which was between the two bedrooms and was only used for such social occasions. In our

European-style house in Cuzco, we would call this the 'parlor' and it served the same purpose. It was only used on more important social occasions. I ventured in there one day and found it a delightful though dark room as Mamma kept the curtains over the two small windows closed to keep out the light and stop the furnishings from fading. There was a large, round table made of a dark red wood that was highly polished. Over this was a lovely white tablecloth which had been finely crocheted. In the centre of this table was a large and finely-crafted oil lamp. In the corner of the room was a large fireplace in the Spanish style with large metal fittings and hooks for hanging pots. To its right, on the wall which adjoined the main bedroom was a large painting showing Jesus and his Sacred Heart. On the opposite wall was a small family shrine on a table with mirrored wings surrounding a statue of the Madonna. There were silken flowers placed at her feet as well as some freshly picked ones in a vase from a few days before. There was also a small chest of drawers with some artifacts sitting on top and above this was a shelf containing even more curiosities. Over the fireplace was a faded likeness of Uncle Guillermo in the uniform of a Sargento in the Liberation Army of José de San Martín."

"That is a very fine house." Garcia said. "Our home in the mountains well to the north of Cuzco was not as grand. We had the usual small farm with a two-story house with only one room upstairs. We would slide a curtain across to give some privacy between us children and Mama and Papa but there was not much space to share. Below were the stalls for the animals. We also had a poor little cow,

Consuela who gave us a little milk. When our family increased in size, my older brother Manuel and I slept in the storeroom which was in the other building housing the small kitchen."

"I continued my story:

After the adults had left, we would join the older children around the big table. There would be small, sweet cakes and jugs of unfermented chicha to drink. Cousin Joachim, really my second cousin, and Cousin Ramone's oldest son who was at least twelve would tell us stories. He told us about the spirits who lived in the mountains. There were the Apu who lived in their own mountains who could be asked for protection when one was going into their domain. Joachim said that the Apu would sometimes appear as large birds with human heads and when camped in the mountains one could hear their wings flapping at night. There were also the mischievous Murki who lived under the ground in caves and especially in mines. They were described as being very short, brown and having long golden hair. They would sometimes come out at night and kidnap unbaptised children to work in their mines and upset any others who invaded their mountains. Joachim said that this was true because his abuelo told him that this is why the Spaniards had left their gold mine at a la Buena Esperanza.

His favourite story was from the Collao people who lived further south near Lake Titicaca. This was about the Anchancho, evil spirits who lived in the mountains and who could enter and take possession of people when their soul - the Jukkui Ajayo - leaves the body in sleep or when a person has a sudden fright. They also possessed the power of the evil eye and could charm a person, then enter their body and then suck their heart's blood causing disease and death. They were particularly active just on twilight. Of course Cousin Joachim would tell this story with great relish and all of us smaller children would be very scared. You can understand that, after drinking large jugs of unfermented chicha, we would be very reluctant to venture outside to the toilet. Later, it would be a very quick rush to my bedroom to hide under the covers!"

"Oh. Si, Señor." Said Garcia. "These I understand. It is the same in northern Peru. My mother would sing us a song if we would not go to sleep:

'Duérmete niño, duérmete ya...

Que viene el Cucuy y te comerá.[11]'

"Yes. Cucuy the Bogyman, who would eat naughty little children." I continued. "My old Aunt Esmeralda would tell me about him when she was caring for me. It frightened me too and so I would pretend to go to sleep. But who can sleep with el Cucuy about?"

Garcia laughed. "Well luckily we grew up, Don Hernán. But still, there were times in the mountains at night when I asked for help from the Apu to protect me from such things"

"I know that too, Garcia." I replied." I have often been up in the mountains

---

[11] Spanish: for 'Sleep child, sleep now...
here comes the Cucuy and he will eat you'

alone at night and feel that perhaps I am not alone. That is where faith is needed.

Well, to continue my story on a happier note: the second week of our stay with Doña Isabella' was the week of the Fiesta of Corpus Christi. It was to be a joyous occasion to honour the holiness of the sacraments. Mother had been helping Doña Isabella all week to prepare the food which we would have after the great procession through the streets of Checacupe. She also helped make the dresses and costumes which we would wear. I had a lovely pair of black trousers, a black shirt and waistcoat and a big red bandana which I would wear around my neck and down over my shoulders. I also had a broad-brimmed black hat with many coloured plumes stuck in its band. I did look handsome."

Garcia laughed even louder, he got up and pranced around in that particular shuffle that was characteristic of the Andean dance. "Oh, you would have looked a fine hombrecito[12], mi Colonel," he said with glee.

"Yes, Garcia." I replied. "I did feel very proud and very happy when I put on my new clothes. Mother made a lovely long pink dress which had many flowers over it. She also had a wide shawl made of fine, white alpaca wool which Doña Isabella had crocheted and a lovely white hat with a broad black band covered in flowers. She looked beautiful and grinned like a little girl when she first put it on.

Because it was a special occasion, Cousin Ramone came in his little cart to take us

12 'Little man'

into the village. Doña Isabella wore the traditional party garb of the district with several wide polleras of red and pink with floral designs, a light brown juyuna or jacket with front panels decorated with animal designs and held together with several bright white buttons. She also wore a colourful red and white striped lliclla fastened at the front with a silver tupu and on her head she had a red upturned monteras with its white chin strap. What a lovely sight they made! Ramone was also in his best clothing. He had wide, baggy black trousers, leather sandals called ajotas and a large poncho made of broad red and white stripes with little designs in many of the bands. On his head he wore a colourful knitted cap called a chullos which had long earflaps down the side and a big white tassel on top. Mother and Doña Isabella sat up on the seat with

Cousin Ramone, whilst I sat on some clean sacks in the back of the cart. It was a great day for the fiesta!

We drove slowly along the road towards the village and passed many people also in their colourful costumes who were walking to the fiesta.

'Hola' many of them would call out, or 'Buenos Dias!'

When we arrived we found the village crowded. Checacupe did not have a grand Plaza de Armes like many of the bigger towns but it had a large walled enclosure with a big archway which was now decorated with flowers. Cousin Ramone parked his little cart near the wall of this enclosure just along from its gate and we walked the short distance down the road to the small church with its single white tower and decorated portico. The bells were calling the people to Mass.

After the mass was over, we joined the people outside who had formed a large group surrounding the steps of the church. We knew soon that the leading men of the Parish would soon be bringing out the Monstrance[13] as well as the statues of Jesus, Mary and the Saints. I was eager to see the grand procession. Of course I had seen one before in Cuzco, but there the crowd had been immense and as a little child I had not seen much. Suddenly the man carrying the large golden Monstrance shaped like a huge sun with many golden rays coming from its centre piece came through the door –

[13] The monstrance, or ostensory is a vessel for the more convenient exhibition of some object of piety, such as the consecrated Eucharistic host.

perhaps this was also a reference to the old god Inti – the sun. Behind him came the first group of men carrying a large statue of Jesus dressed in the finest robes made especially for this occasion and mounted on a platform of wood supported by two long poles which the men in their best black suits carried on their shoulders. There was a large cry from the watching crowd and near the steps a group of musicians dressed in traditional garb began to play their panpipes or zampoñas, flutes and drums to lead the procession down the road to the enclosure. The Alcalde with his large red sash of office and a broad white sombrero had mounted his big white horse to take his place in the front of the procession. Many people threw flowers in the path of the procession or onto the statues themselves. Some even ran to the platforms of the statues to kiss the base asking for a blessing from a particular occupant. We joined in with the rest of the crowd and walked behind. Many people were also dancing as this was a happy event.

The procession moved down the main street of the village then turned at the intersection into the road which ran from the highway to the river and then on to Paucartambo. After a short distance it turned into the enclosure, whilst the main body of the parade – the Alcalde, the band and the church officials with the statues continued into the middle of the compound. The rest of us moved in and around the inside wall. Inside, the main body moved around the compound in a huge circle so that all could see and venerate the statues. After several circuits, the main body left the enclosure to return to the church where the statues would be placed around the portico. Some of the more faithful followed this body, but the rest stayed within the walls of the enclosure. A group of bare-headed young men in black trousers with white shirts ran into the centre carrying a large pole which was festooned with streamers. This was a Maypole. I was intrigued by the way the men had planted the pole and then secured it with guy-ropes to the ground. Next came a group of ladies and young girls in dresses, shawls and hats which were mainly of white and pink. They formed a group in the centre where they danced in a rhythmic way around the pole intertwining themselves through the streamers which came from the top of the pole. A group of men in orange pantaloons, black jackets and tall plumed black hats entered and danced in a circle around the pole but outside of the women's circle. On their faces they wore grotesque black masks. All of the time the band played their haunting tunes on the shrill, throaty pipes and a multitude of rhythmic beating drums.

After the maypole dances came four riders mounted on white horses which were covered in large, white cloths covering most of their bodies under the saddle. The men wore black pants with coats and tall hats with numerous plumes just like mine. After this, pairs of men and women in their bright, traditional costumes formed a procession which danced around the outer edge of compound. When this group passed by, the bystanders joined the end of the procession and we all danced slowly back to the church in the village. Here the priest came out onto the portico and blessed the waiting crowd before it dispersed to the many stalls which had been set up along the main street. Here, they were offering for sale a great variety of foods, drinks, clothing and trinkets to celebrate the fiesta.

What a great day we had! Mother was back in her youth: she danced; and laughed; and was happy. I too, had had a wonderful day. It was like a new beginning; the joy of these simple country folk; the love and care which they openly shared with much generosity, gave my soul new life.

The last week passed very quickly. There had been many visits to Mother's other relatives nearby and the making of many new friends. I was allowed to wander freely around the farm; playing with other children whilst their mothers worked in the fields; looking for the eggs of our chickens in the long grass near the house and watching Mamma milk Ana the cow. Soon it was time to leave the house on the road to Good Hope. Cousin Ramone arrived early in the morning and carried our bags down to his little cart. Mamma and Mother sat up with him and I enjoyed my last ride sitting on the boards in the back. When we arrived in the village at the posada where we were to meet the coach from Puno, there were a large number of people. All of my mother's cousins and friends whom we had met over the last few weeks were there. All were both happy and sad. Some of the women had tears in their eyes but smiles on their faces. It had been a happy stay and now the people were here to wish us a safe trip. There were also little baskets of fruit, dried potatoes and corn and other little gifts for us. In time the coach was pulled out of the Posada where the horses were harnessed up. The other passengers emerged, sleepy-eyed from their rooms –

remember that Checacupe was an overnight coaching stop – and we gave Mamma and Cousin Ramone a last embrace before we climbed up to our seats.

'Via con Dios!'[14] different people shouted and the coach slowly rolled out of the village, Mother leaning out of the window and waving her handkerchief.

Well, Garcia, that is my little story of el camino a la Buena Esperanza. Was it any help to you?"

"Oh, mi Colonel, it was a beautiful story," he said. It has brought back so many good memories of my carefree childhood, my home and all of my family and friends who lived there. Thank you.

[14] 'Go with God!'

I feel much better now and it has put me back onto my own road to good hope."

"Good! You sound almost like a philosopher." I laughed. "So let us both have hope that soon we will be returned to our families and friends. Whilst Inti the sun shines on our faces and God is in our hearts there is always hope."

El décimo carta - la Ejecución

(The tenth letter - the execution)

My dearest wife and children.

This will be my last letter from San Rafael. It is a pity really, for I have enjoyed telling these tales of the people here and elsewhere and some of their stories. I find now that words about our situation have failed me for it is the unhappiest day of my life.

This day began like all of the others at San Rafael. There was the usual knock on my door about seven and usually it would be unlocked and Ambrosio, the Comandante's general factotum would enter with the morning coffee. Today, however it was the Comandante himself dressed in his dressing gown and slippers and he bore a long letter in his hand. His face was one of sadness masked by the set expression of the soldier when faced with a bad situation.

"I will not say 'buenos dias', Don Hernán for it is not a good day for us all," he said as he waved the letter above his head. "This letter comes from the Junta in Quito. It is your death warrant and my retirement. They consider you a difficult political prisoner and your capture and presence in Ecuador is a big embarrassment to them. So the easiest solution is to quietly remove all trace of you and your men"

He sat on the end of my bed and looked a tired old man. "This letter orders me to execute you and your men upon the arrival of one Capitán Carrasco Flores who will observe that these orders are carried out. He, no doubt, is one of the Junta's favourites and looking for fast promotion for it is a dishonourable task and I know of no officer of my past acquaintance who would knowingly carry it out."

I had no words for this and just sat in my bed and looked back at the Comandante. His eyes were red with the tears he must have had when he first opened the letter for he is a good and honourable man.

"It also contains direction for the end of my career, not that this is important at this time. I find it totally unpleasant to have to carry out such a despicable order at its end. There came in this same dispatch, which arrived by horseman last night, my 'Honourable Discharge'. What an oxymoron is this expression now. I had looked forward to such a document but now it fades in importance. I am to be retired after many long years of service, many battles both large and small and, as you can see, many scars and one arm in the service of my country. Well, at least my value, if not my honour has been recognised by the Junta for they also sent a sizeable amount of gold coin as my pension and in recognition of my 'special services'. A bribe is still a bribe in any words, huh, Don Hernán?"

I climbed out of the bed and put on the robe which had been given to me when we had first arrived.

"And my men, Antonio?" I said. "What is to become of them?"

The old Comandante smiled at my use of his first name. We had become friends over these many weeks and now was not a test of that.

"I am sorry, Hernán, but they too are to be executed – simply removed as unwanted vermin. The letter says as much as that. You are to be accorded a proper firing squad as is appropriate to an enemy of the State – perhaps the Junta believes that they are honourable men doing this – but you men, the Sargento and the two who will be brought from the hospital are to be 'quietly removed.' I am sorry. I am still a soldier and must carry out these orders. To let you and your men go in defiance of them would be my first choice if I knew that no one else is affected. Unfortunately my sense of duty and the safety of my people both here and in Quito is also a consideration. I am sorry."

"Thank you Antonio," I replied. "That is that, then. There is nothing more to do. May I be permitted however to write to my family and tell them of the last acts of my men and I?"

"That would not be allowed by the Junta, you understand," said the Comandante with a solemn face" But another 'letter from San Rafael' is probably in order. I think."

I looked at him in surprise and he smiled at my reaction.

"Oh do not be alarmed, Hernán. I have known of your letters from the first one which your Sargento had handed to Luis not long after your arrival here. He like all of my people here are like little children. I know as soon as they tell me a tale and they do not lie when I asked them. They still keep to the Incan code up here in the mountains, and lying is not in their nature, so I let them pass on the letters to their cousins which they do so like little children sharing a secret from their father. For to them, that is what I have become. This time, for their sake, I will give the letter to Fray Dominic who is as much a member of our big family as he is my friend and a good man. He will come also to give you any spiritual assistance you may need when the day arrives. Unfortunately, I have been ordered to keep you under lock-and-key and your Sargento also. I will ask Doctor Ernesto to bring your other men from his hospital and then make the usual, unpleasant pronouncements. Forgive me."

With that he quickly stood up and left the room. The door was locked behind him and I was left with my emptiness and my thoughts. The day passed very quickly, not because I was occupied in some absorbing task but simply because I was often lost in thought. I remembered my childhood. My home in Cuzco and my wife and children. All of those little episodes which one forgets so easily. Games with the children. Coming home to a warm fire and embraces with my family. One gets so involved with the daily tasks and routines of life that the important things are often put aside. I remember too, my early days as a student and young academic. The pride and the arrogance of university life; how study was all consuming, leaving little time for the simpler enjoyments of life. It seemed as though I had spent too much time reading other peoples' writings about life without living my own life to the full. And there was my military life which took up so much of my family's life and now is the end of mine. What started out as a simple act of support for my poor conscripted friends had become a passion. I had wanted to compete with the other officers yet I did not want to be part of all of their bluster about the glory and honour of war and of national pride. There have been many times when I have envied Garcia's simple faith and view of life. My world was one of grey shadows; Garcia's world was full of light and sharp contrasts. A person to him was either good or bad; each day brought fresh thoughts. I lived in a world of gradation; everything was looked at carefully and there were no clear edges, just differences in shade. For Garcia, God was in Heaven where he looked down upon the faithful. Children were born and people died. Life was that simple. The sun came up and the people went to work in the fields or on the barrack drill square. Everything was simple. I drifted in and out of faith, wondering whether this doctrine was a true law of God or simply a pronouncement of power from those who controlled the Church. The thoughts of people like me are often weighed in the balance like the grains of the trader at the market place. In the end I had set myself apart and came to my own conclusions that God was a personal entity which existed inside everyone, and everything around me was His creation. This also determined my fate so why did I have remorse for the things which I would like to have done now that my time was ending?

I felt for poor Garcia locked in his little room below. Perhaps he was in a better mind than I! He would have taken the Comandante's news and condolences with a good heart and with some fatality as is the way with many of the people of the mountains. Fate is fate. It is what guides people like Garcia so he would have accepted that his life was now to end. He would have had much sadness because he would not see his wife and children. He would have wanted to again work the fields each day below his beloved snowy mountains and return home at the end of the day to his little warm house in the valley and be greeted by his smiling wife and laughing children. Oh, how I wish for the simple life where thoughts guide rather than confuse!

The sun is setting now and from the doorway of my little balcony I can see a small, emerald hummingbird in the sparse tree which has grown from the cliff face on which the hacienda sits. It is delicate with an iridescent green body and blue head. It darts here and there seeking nectar in the few blooms which have lasted this long. Beyond is the narrow valley which has been cut by the Rio Pastaza gurgling its way down finally into the Amazon below. The greens of the steep slopes are darker now and I feel sleep approaching like the darkness outside.

I only regret that I could not see you before I go; and the smiling, innocent faces of the children. I have spent too long taking about the words of others so that now I find it difficult to find my own. Remember me as a man who tried to do his best and loved you all, even at times when my thoughts were elsewhere. Please take care of the children and also look to Garcia's wife Constanzia and her children too, for Garcia has been my mainstay in the struggles of the real world. Also, please give whatever assistance you can to the families of our other two men who have suffered much with their wounds and now will have their lives ended. They are Soldado de Primera Pedro Álvares Muñoz and Soldado Enrique Ernesto Garrido Marín. I cannot write anymore. I am like the student studying all his life for that one final exam. I have done what I can and now I am in the hands of God. Farewell.

Hernán

Señora Moreno, please forgive. It is I, García writing. My letters are not so good. I have little time. Fray Dominic is here to help me to God. He has given me Don Hernán's letter to add my own words. I must tell you that the bad capitán from Quito allowed me to watch. Don Hernán died quickly and with honour like a soldier. I saw Sargento Pérez – a good man – bring the Colonel out and walking to the far wall of the courtyard. His hands were tied behind. The soldiers of the hacienda marched in and formed a line. They looked good – for a change. Like soldiers should. Teniente Rivera with his sword drawn walked over to Don Hernán and offered him a blindfold. It was refused. He marched back then inspected the line of his soldiers. Each one he inspected. Finally he retired to the end of the line and gave the orders. Present! Fire! Don Hernán fell quickly. Fray Dominic rushed over to his body and said a quiet prayer. Doctor Ernesto came and said that he was dead. Then Luis and Miguel carried the body away. All here were in tears as they loved your husband. As did I! They come for me now and I must go to God also. Please give my love to my wife and my

children and if you can look after them
and those of our men. Viva Peru!

Pedro Garcia Lorca
Sargento Primera

Do not be distressed, my darling for I am not dead yet! Neither is Garcia nor our two men. I think it was the American humorist Mark Twain who said a few years ago that 'The report of my death was an exaggeration'. I am sorry that I have given you the news of my apparent resurrection as an addition to my first writing rather than in a new and perhaps happier letter. I was much taken by the note from Garcia and by the honesty which I expressed when I was faced with death. Please forgive me and I must explain:

What Garcia said was true. The faithful Sargento of Comandante Castillo, Pérez called for me in the morning and with great apologies tied my hands behind my back. His face was set in the expressionless mask of the professional soldier and his uniform was immaculate. His bearing and uniform were at odds to the more casual soldier to which I had been accustomed. I was taken out into the courtyard and stood facing outwards. Up on the balcony was the Comandante, the insipid-looking Capitán from Cuzco who was obviously enjoying the spectacle and my faithful Garcia – solid as ever and ramrod straight. He gave me a little salute as if to say 'farewell, mi Colonel' which I could hear within my head. Despite my feelings of self-pity and fatality, I was surprised when the soldiers of the hacienda were marched in. Their uniforms were clean and tidy; their hair cut short and their weapons polished. They marched with precision and pride with their heads held high – although I did notice that some had tears on their brown cheeks. Teniente Rivera Peña also looked smart and held himself like a soldier with his bright sword vertical in his hand as he marched over to me. He held a bright red bandana in his other hand, my blindfold I assumed.

Rivera marched right up to me so that his face was very close to me. He looked into my eyes and I saw some doubt in his. He offered me the blindfold and I refused. Then he said something which I will remember for the rest of my days.

"For the love of God and all of our sake, fall down as though you are dead when the rifles fire. There will be sometime when you must lay still. Do not move when you have fallen, I beg of you, please Colonel. God be with us all." He said and turned smartly to march back to his men.

These words were a shock to me. I kept my face expressionless as I watched him dress and then inspect the firing line of his troops. They looked smart and he had no doubt ordered that they be their best for this ceremony - for my sake rather than the fool from Quito. The Teniente walked down the line of the men who stood at attention, inspecting each man and talking to each in turn. When he had completed his inspection he continued past the end of the line. Then raised his sword into the air and gave the orders quickly – 'Present, Fire!'

The levelled rifles fired with a defining but unified sound. 'A good volley' I thought for a split second and then I heard the thuds of the bullets striking the wall around me and the wind of some passing my ears. No bullets struck me and I jerked and fell down as though I had been struck. I lay there motionless and felt the presence of someone knelling over me, his shadow upon me. A small prayer came softly from Fray Dominic's lips:

"In nomine patris et filii et spiritus sancti – stay still Don Hernán, it is not time for your resurrection yet - benedicat nos hodie hic actus bonus et potens poteris. Amen," he said then stood up and left, probably making a big show of making the sign of the cross.

Next I felt another presence and felt two fingers on the side of my neck. "He is dead," pronounced Doctor Ernesto who also quickly retired.

There was some delay and I heard some faint clapping in the distance – that of only a single man. No doubt the vain Capitán Carrasco thought that my death was worthy of applause. I hoped that he accepted my performance. There also were the soft cries and wailing of some of the womenfolk of the hacienda who had gathered around the edge of the courtyard after the soldiers had departed to continue their morning rituals with Garcia and my other two men. I Prayed to God silently that they would meet the same fate as I.

Soon, I felt my body being lifted gently - hands under my arms and around my legs. "I am sorry if we are too rough, Don

Hernán," came the quiet voice of Luis, the wagon driver. I was carried a few steps across the courtyard and gently placed on the tray of the wagon. A rough military blanket was thrown over my body and Luis begged me to lie still and wait until it was lifted.

I felt the wagon lurch as the two men climbed up on to the seat and the movement of the wagon as it slowly passed out of the courtyard and down the road. It seemed that time was standing still below that blanket. Despite the early hour, it was hot and I was tempted to raise the cover but I remembered the sincerity of all of the advice given to me so I remained still. I almost sat straight up when I heard another volley of shots off in the distance. This was the firing squad in action again and I prayed once more for the salvation of my men.

Soon the wagon rattled off the road with a bump and I felt it slowing bouncing along a rough track. We stopped and Luis threw off the blanket and with a big grin helped me to sit upright and gave me a huge embrace.

"Welcome back, Colonel Hernán. Forgive me that I should be so happy." He said with tears running down his broad, honest face.

I looked around and there running down to the wagon was Garcia, his face streaming with tears. "Don Hernán, Don Hernán," he cried. "We are all alive! Thanks be to God."

A little way off being sheltered in the trees were our other two men with Doctor Ernesto and the soldiers of the firing squad. Sargento Pérez was there also with a broad grin on his face. The soldiers and my two men under the trees had cups in their hands and there was a barrel of the Comandante's good wine sitting on a tree stump.

"Come and join us, Don Hernán," said Doctor Ernesto. "Your death must have been very tiring!" The men laughed at this and I eased myself off the end of the wagon and walked up the hill.

"We must stay here hidden for a while, Colonel Moreno," said Sargento Pérez "until the coach of the thin Capitán from the Junta has left. I have one of my best riders up on the hill from which he can see the road almost to Baños and he will come and tell us when it is safe to return to the hacienda."

While we waited, we all enjoyed the stillness in the coolness of the thick grove of trees. Doctor Ernesto expressed his feelings by saying that for once he was not ashamed that his diagnoses of my death was incorrect. He was, however proud that his ministrations to my two men in his little hospital had been successful and that they were fit enough to travel – they had recovered well from their deaths also. Soon, a mounted soldier reigned his horse up beyond the trees and ran up to report to Sargento Pérez who turned to us and told us that it was all clear. My men were helped up onto the wagon and Garcia and I followed. Sargento Pérez formed up his men who once more looked a fine military squad. We started off back up the road to Baños and the hacienda. Our firing squad marched proudly behind the wagon in two lines, rifles with bayonets fixed and singing part of their National Anthem"

"Nadie, oh Patria, lo intente. Las sombras
de tus héroes gloriosos nos miran
y el valor y el orgullo que inspiran
son augurios de triunfos por ti.
Venga el hierro y el plomo fulmíneo,
que a la idea de guerra y venganza
se despierta la heroica pujanza
que hizo al fiero español sucumbir"[1].

[1] The lyrics were written in 1865 by the poet Juan León Mera:
"No one, oh fatherland, tries it.
The shadows of Your glorious heroes watch us,
And the value and pride that inspire
They are omens of victories for you.
Come lead and the striking iron,

When our little procession reached the hacienda, both gates were thrown open and all of the people ran out to greet us. They had tears in their eyes and hats and scarves were being waved. They all shouted welcome and walked along with us through the gates.

Standing in the middle of the outer courtyard was the Comandante. He was in his full dress uniform with plumed Kepi[2] and his sword was raised in front of his face in salute. As we drew near, he quickly swung his sword down sharply and out to his right hand side, completing the salute of honour. He

> That the idea of war and revenge
> Wakes the heroic strength
> That made the fierce Spanish succumb."

[2] A round, soft military cap with a horizontal peak.

sheathed his sword and briskly walked toward the now stationary wagon.

"Greetings my friends!" he said. "Welcome to the Hacienda San Rafael"

Indeed as I looked around it was as though the tired old hacienda had also come to life. No longer a neglected old building of crumbling brown walls, but now bright and proud with coloured cloths hanging from the windows and balconies and streamers running from one corner to the next. Tables were being set up around the walls and the civilian staff was dressed in their best clothes. All of the soldiers now were in their best uniforms and it was time for celebration.

The Comandante came forward and embraced me, kissing me on both cheeks. "Come, Hernán. We have much to talk about and some apologies on my part. Your Sargento and you men will be cared for and my people are preparing a great fiesta in celebration of your – shall we say your 'untimely death?'

The Comandante and I walked upstairs to the main room where we found Teniente Rivera seated in front of the fireplace. He stood up quickly and said "Welcome back, Colonel Morano. I am so glad that your death was convincing."
"Thank you, I replied. "It was not easy but I had faith in your marksmen." I laughed.

"Yes, Colonel," he said with a grin. "I chose four of my best marksmen to just miss your head. They did very well considering that the men were only told of the plot whilst I was inspecting their line. It came as a very happy surprise when I ordered all of them to miss. I think that there must have been some further competition between my marksmen to see who could shoot the closest. Alejandro was sure that he had nicked your ear and sends his apologies."

"Ha! It was lucky for him that he missed!" I said. "But you can tell your four shooters that I felt the wind of their bullets very close indeed."

We had sat down in the Comandante's comfortable chairs and he poured three glasses of his best wine, giving them to me, Teniente Rivera and myself. "Well!" He said. "I must give you the full story. You can appreciate that we have all become good friends here at San Rafael. You and your Sargento and my people, of course, who are like my own family. It came as a devastating blow to receive those hated orders from the Junta in Quito. They panicked that your capture would lead to further escalation of the border tensions so they had to get rid of the evidence. I am just an old soldier of a previous age when honour and not deception was the done thing – but then you are an Exploring Officer who rides around in full uniform looking for your enemies and hoping that your fast horse will save you from capture. It was too bad you went on foot with your patrol, but then you would not have been my guest. Fate makes strange friends.

Well, to my story. Having read and then re-read those hateful orders, and having paced these boards many times I decided that honour exceeded duty so I called for Gabriel here and we came up with our little plot. That was true, was it not Gabriel?"

"Oh, si mi Comandante," it was like I was back in school in Ushuaia plotting with my friends how to get out of lessons and go climbing in the mountains." He replied and it was a mark of the new faith and confidence that this young man now had that his superior would use his Christian name.

"So," the Comandante continued. We decided to have honour and do our duties. So how could we execute you as well as maintain our honour as decent soldiers. We enlisted the aid of the indomitable Fray Dominic who is a good man and was once an honourable soldier. We needed him to keep you quiet after your apparent death. And of course, Doctor Ernesto was overjoyed at his role in the play. The others in the hacienda were not told of the plot until it was their turn to act. Luis, I told just before the execution and poor Gabriel here had only a few minutes to give new orders to his men when they were lined in the firing squad. It was a mark of their faith in men and the trust in this brave officer here that they were able to carry out your execution without fuss. The poor ladies who watched, of course did not know of our plans and I was both appreciative of their genuine sorrow and sad for my deception. Tonight I will give all of my people an apology although by now they would have heard the story from their men."

"So what will happen now?" I asked.

"Oh, we will continue to obey the Junta's orders, of course." He laughed. In a few days you and your men will be placed back on the wagon and taken back to where you were found. But this time, the disagreeable Capitán Moralez and his wild Jivaros will not be there to greet you, for things are now quiet again on the frontier and they have been transferred further north into the jungle to harass the poor natives there. Although I feel somewhat unhappy about Moralez because the tribes up there are related to the Jiveros and no matter how civilised they are and wear a uniform, these people tend to look after themselves and individuals mistrust each other in the deep jungle. Anyway, that is no longer your concern.

The wagon will be stocked for a good trip with comfortable mattresses, tents and plenty of food and drink. You and your men, and I daresay Luis and Miguel will also enjoy themselves because you will have a good supply of wine and beer

– and my best cigars which you have often enjoyed! I am sorry to say that this journey will not get you home before your letter which Fray Dominic will take to the traders up in the mountains, but we must be cautious and go the long way around. Past where you were first found, the road climbs back up into the mountains and eventually meets the main road south into your country. As you may know, from what I was told, the border guards are all related to some of my people here and some of the coins from the Junta will no doubt ensure a safe passage and silence. We will take you to Nambale just across the border. It is a long way and will probably take many days but you will be safe. I will send my own letter by the fast post to the border which will go on to your family within the week, so they will know that you are coming."

"And what about you and your people?" I asked with some concern.

"Oh that is also the good news." He replied with a gleam in his eyes. "I have orders from the Junta itself – not from my Headquarters in Ambato –to close down and remove all traces of this supply depot and to reassign all of my people. For the young Teniente here, who really wants to be a lawyer, I have already signed his transfer papers to the Judge Advocate General's office in Quito where he can complete his studies and then spend the rest of his life tangling up the military in legal jargon. My older soldiers who have families nearby will receive their long-awaited honourable discharges with pensions and the rest of my soldiers will be transferred to places near their homes, although I fear that many of the younger ones will desert. It is the way of a conscript army, but they will have some money and supplies to take with them back to their farms."

We all laughed at that and the Teniente thanked the Comandante again for his kindness.

"As for me!" the Comandante continued "I will be retired. I have this new pension – plus the extra money of, course which I will share with all of my people here and some for Fray Dominic to distribute amongst his flock. I have been asked many times by my daughter to go to her home in Colombia to be with her and my several grandchildren so I can be the grumpy old abuelo. I will have no problems with my Headquarters as they have been told to be silent by their superiors. I shall ride in my carriage in style with the goodwill of all the people here and in Baños - I think that Fray Dominic and the Alcalde have some plans for a farewell. Then I will take the main road down to Guayaquil and take the steamer north to Tumaco in Colombia, not far from my daughter's estancia. I am not worried about the Junta in Quito well to my north. The good Capitán will no doubt give a glowing report on my last command, including of course his magnificent role in the proceedings. Besides, I feel from what is being said around my circle of trusted friends in Quito, the Junta will not last very long.

As for this old hacienda – well. She has had a long life although rather shabby and forlorn until today. Much like its Comandante, huh, Gabriel? We have many stores here and also many poor people in the district. As a token I will send all of the weapons, ammunition, items of uniform and other military paraphernalia back to Headquarters at Ambato, but everything else here will be distributed to my people and those in the district. There is a considerable amount of building material, household wares and, of course much food and wine. Everyone here will feel themselves to be rich. But more than that - they will leave with honour. For this we have to thank you, Don Hernán" he said with a formal bow.

So that is my final story – it has been a great adventure: at times sad and at others happy. I have made many friends here amongst my country's enemies which shows that we share more in common than that we have in disagreement. Perhaps there may be a time when people will talk first before

firing the first shot and when we can all
live in peace with our neighbours.

So this is my last letter from San Rafael.
Adios!

About the Author

Hernán Eduardo Moreno Ruiz is, like this story fictional. Had he really lived one would find that he was born in Cuzco, Peru about 1844, the only son of Don Bernardo Moreno Fuentes, a minor politician and Doña Valentina Sisa Yupanqui who could trace her ancestry back to the Incan nobility. His father died when Hernán was about five years old and he was raised by his mother with the help of her family in reduced circumstances. He was admitted to the Universidad Nacional de San Antonio Abad del Cuzco and went on to achieve his Doctorate and a position as lecturer in the Philosophy Faculty. In addition, he volunteered for the part-time Militia and was commissioned into a local infantry regiment, becoming an 'Exploring Officer' – an independent intelligence gatherer. It was on his last mission with his faithful Sargent Pedro Garcia Lorca and a small patrol that he was captured by a unit of the Ecuadoran Army then sent to the fortified hacienda at San Rafael.

About the Compiler of this Book

Although given as the compiler of these letters, Dr. Peter Terrence Scott is the actual author using the non de plume of Hernán Moreno Ruiz. He has many similarities to his fictional hero; raised and educated in Sydney, Australia, then graduating as a nineteen-year-old Science Teacher to begin a successful career of over forty years in high schools and universities. Studying at various universities part time, he achieved a Bachelor of Science, Masters Degrees in Science (Geology) and Educational Administration and a Doctorate in Education. He too volunteered for the Army Reserve in support of his friends who had been conscripted during the Vietnam War and was commissioned into the infantry.

After retiring from teaching he has visited all seven continents including South America several times. Here he and his wife travelled extensively visiting, his daughter-in-law's family in the high Andes and also many of the places mentioned in this book.

He now lives in Brisbane, Australia with his wife and their sons and families including five grandchildren. He is the author of nine books on Earth Science, the Adventures in Earth Science series.

Dr Scott at Baños de Agua Santa, 2011